BEAU

Sheppard's Shadow Book 5

KATHI S. BARTON

This is a work of fiction. Names, characters, places, and incidents are products of the author's imagination or are used fictitiously and are not to be construed as real. Any resemblance to actual events, locations, organizations, or persons, living or dead, is entirely coincidental.

World Castle Publishing, LLC
Pensacola, Florida
Copyright © 2025 Kathi S. Barton
Hardback ISBN: 9798267391573
Paperback ISBN: 9798891264779
eBook ISBN: 9798891264786
First Edition World Castle Publishing, LLC, October 6, 2025
http://www.worldcastlepublishing.com

Cover: Cover Designs by Karen
Editor: Karen Fuller

Chapter 1

Rogen felt better than she had in a while—it was because there wasn't as much stress on her, and she was getting enough sleep too. Rolling out of bed, she took a quick shower and decided that since she had messed up the picnic yesterday evening, she'd go see Weston in his office and break a few pieces of furniture while playing around with him. Almost as soon as she closed the door to his office—telling Belinda to go away, she sat on his desk with the food and fed him grapes while telling him what she was going to do to him, in as much detail as she could think of.

"First things first, I'm going to feed you so that you have plenty of strength to fuck me." He took the grapes from her and nearly choked trying to get them in his mouth. "You idiot. Don't kill yourself. We have the rest of the day to have some fun."

"What kind of fun did you want to have? I'm all for it, no matter what it was." She told him that she wanted him right there on his desk. "My pleasure. I just have a few things to move here so that we don't break them, especially not my computer. Then I plan on breaking you into lots of pieces."

Putting his laptop on the floor, he moved the picnic basket beside it. As his movements were slow, she could feel her pussy getting wetter by the moment. When he put his hand on her legs, she was so glad she'd worn a dress. It made things much easier for the two of them. Then he planted her feet onto the arms of his chair. As he held them there, stroking the inside of her ankle, all she could think about was him having her any way that he wanted.

Weston moved his hands up under her dress slowly to her thighs, then he pulled her panties off. Being slightly disappointed that he'd not gotten to see them, she was satisfied that he could smell her; she could smell herself, that spike of need was taking her breath away. It was all she could do not to pull him to her and have him eat her. When he asked her to lie back on the desk, Rogen did as he asked and waited. She didn't have long to wait as he buried his mouth over her and suckled at her pussy, bringing her up off the desk quickly, only to be pushed back down by his gentle hands.

"I'm not nearly finished with you yet. That was only the start of my having you." She said that she'd come. "Good, more for me. Now lie back and enjoy what I'm doing to you."

The climax took her breath away. It had hit her hard and consumed her. Even as Weston fucked her with his tongue, she held onto the sides of the desk and enjoyed herself. Christ, he was good at this, and she didn't want it to ever end.

She came so many times, hard climaxes that took her breath away, to small short releases that seemed to come from the bottom of her feet to her head that made her skin tingle. She was left feeling like she couldn't go on, wanting more from him so that she could hit the epic climax that would render her unconscious. Rogen wanted it all.

Putting her legs up and over his shoulders, Rogen rode his mouth, using her hips and legs to do so. His tongue was doing all kinds of things to her pussy, fucking her and licking her from gate to clit. She came so many times that she didn't know if she'd survive. Weston slid one of his fingers into her pussy, and she nearly came up off the desk. Grabbing a handful of his hair, she pressed him tighter against her and begged him for more.

Rogen was limp with her releases after about ten minutes of him eating her, and didn't know if she could handle even one more. She could barely move when Weston stood up. She thought for sure that he was finished with her, so she tried to sit up to touch him. Instead, he worked his pants open and teased her pussy with his cock. It was too much, and she begged him to stop. But all he did was slam his cock deep within her, making her heart stop beating and her breath taken away.

She came screaming his name. Reaching up to hold onto him, she was delighted when he leaned over her and took her mouth. She could taste herself on his lips, and it was delicious. Even as he fucked her, slowly like he was trying to torture her, she knew that deep in her heart that when she came with him, she was going to come apart, holding onto the only man that she would ever love.

He abused her breasts, her nipples, and her throat with his mouth. As he suckled at her breasts, he nibbled too at her nipples, making them hard and painfully full feeling. Rogen wanted more from him, everything that he could give her, and she knew that if asked, he would give her the moon. But for now, all she wanted was him and all that he could give her.

Wrapping her legs around his waist, he filled her more. Tightening her pussy around him, she heard his moan of pleasure just as she was starting to feel like her body was readying for a release, she held onto him. As he fucked her harder, quicker with each stroke, feeling like it was hitting her in the back of the throat, her body readied for what was to come. When he stiffened and threw back his head, she marveled at the sight of him coming as he growled deep in his body. Christ, she nearly forgot to come watching him in all his glory. When she came then, her body bowing back on the desk, Rogen blacked out just as Weston was telling her that he was coming again.

When she woke, she was on his lap, his cock still deep inside of her while he held her. He was breathing hard, as hard as she was, and it was wonderful. It also made her realize that she'd not been out all that long. Just a few seconds. Tightening her arms around him, he kissed her on the mouth and asked her if she was all right.

"I'm not sure." He laughed a little and said he was feeling the same way, like the rug had been pulled out from under him and he'd had the most delightful time. "I feel like I've been turned inside out. Then turned the other way until it just wore me out. I wonder if us making love will forever be like this. If so, I'm going to be old before my time."

"I'm feeling like that, too. I love you, Rogen Sheppard." She kissed him, a quick kiss on the mouth as he held her. "I hope you brought food with you. I skipped lunch today to do some banking, and I could eat a horse."

They dined on the food that she'd brought. It wasn't nearly enough, so they ordered takeout and had it delivered to their home. On the way there, walking as they both enjoyed the outdoors when they could get it, she told him how her day had begun, and he told her about the check he'd had transferred to Belinda. She thought that she'd cry. She'd married such a wonderful person in Weston. And she couldn't believe that she hadn't wanted anything to do with him at the beginning.

For his help in finding and the arrest of the Hathaways, who had robbed the city blind when he'd been mayor, he'd gotten a personal reward from the Federal Government. It had been just under five hundred thousand dollars for him. Knowing that Belinda, Rogen's sister-in-law, could use the money more than he could, he transferred the money to her account so that she'd have it instead of him. She'd lost her entire family because of a member of her family, and he felt like she deserved it more than he did.

The food arrived just as they were getting out of the hot tub. Having it delivered at six when they wanted it had been perfect. Her body wasn't nearly as sore as she'd been walking home, but she was happy, too. The tub had done them both a great deal of good. Now all they had to do was eat and enjoy the rest of the evening together. It was just the way she thought couples did an early night of debauchery.

After eating their dinner, the two of them sat on the couch and read the newspaper. It didn't take all that long; there were only about four pages of it, and most of it had to do with the sports around town. And being fall in a small town, there was plenty of sports to go around. She found herself dozing off just as the clock was chiming for nine o'clock and she was ready for bed. Getting a good night's sleep was paramount after spending some good fucking time in his office, she thought with a laugh. She might have to take him lunch more often if she felt like this at the end of the day.

Laughing, she made her way to bed with Weston. They both had plenty to do and to take care of, but she thought that she could stand it better if they were to take time for each other instead of catching little bits of time when they could manage it. The evening had been perfect, and she couldn't have been happier if she'd been able to spend a week in bed with Weston. This is what she had wanted all along. To be loved and taken care of by the man that she loved.

At midnight, she heard the phone ringing. It wasn't any ring that she knew, so she let it go. Getting up to go to the bathroom, she looked to see who it was and noticed that it was an unknown number. Putting the phone back on the stand, she did her business and headed back to bed. However, just as she was lying down, it rang again. Picking it up, she decided that at one in the morning, she didn't need to be nice.

"You'd better have a good reason for calling me at this hour. If not, then I'm going to hunt you down and —" The caller said she was her mother. "My mother is gone, thanks for bringing that up. She died about ten years ago now."

"I didn't actually die, but was in a coma. Your father told them to tell you that." She didn't know whether or not to believe her. Then she started spouting off things that only she would know. Or someone who had done a good background check on her. "Do you believe me now?"

"No. I don't know who this is, but surely you could have called at a better hour than one in the morning." She told her that she'd only just arrived in town. "Good for you. If you are my mother, which I still don't believe that you are, you know that I'm a very hard-working person who needs to be in bed by ten to get up at an ungodly hour to work. Who is this really?"

"My name is Glenda Watson. I've been looking for you and your brothers and sister for the last three months. If not for the advertisement in the paper, I might well still be looking." Lying down, snuggling next to Weston as he asked her who it was, she told him that someone saying she was her mother was calling. He, too, couldn't believe it was now that she decided to call. "What will it take for you to believe that I'm your mother? I don't know what else to tell you. You're not being the least bit nice to me. I deserve respect."

"Respect? I don't think so. Call back tomorrow at a decent hour. I'm not saying that I'll believe you any more than I do right now, but I know that I'm pissed off because of the time and the fact that you were supposed to have died nearly ten years ago. Where is Dad in all this? I heard too that he's gone to another country just to deal with his grief. Nothing you can say will change my mind at this hour. Call back tomorrow."

Hanging up on her mom gave her a satisfaction that she'd never felt before. Rogen had never gotten along with her mom, her father, either, for that matter, but telling her that she was still alive when she'd gone to her funeral with the rest of her family just wasn't cutting it. Awake now, she got out of bed and made her way downstairs to look up on the computer about her mother's death. She knew all the details but wanted to make sure that she'd not missed anything back then.

Her mom had been in a car accident while driving drunk. Something that she'd never thought of until right now was that it would have taken a great deal of alcohol to get her mom drunk, as she was a shifter too, but at the time, she or any of the others had thought about that. Their mother had been drinking since they were born and didn't really think about how much it would take for her to be drunk enough to have an accident and for it to have killed her. It just didn't make any sense as to why she'd come around now.

If she remembered correctly, it had been Calhoun who had notified them of her death. She thought about waking him up to see what he had to say, but just as she was convincing herself that this was all a scam for some reason, her brother called her.

"I just heard from someone telling me that she was our mom." She told him that she'd gotten the same call just a little while ago. "I hung up on her. I don't know what sort of scam this is, but I'm not playing with her. Mom died, the insurance policies that we had paid off. We went to the funeral and had a party in her honor. Who is this person who is trying to cause trouble? I don't believe for a minute that it's our mom. Especially after all this time. What's it been, about ten years?"

"Did you actually tell her that we had a party in her honor? And yes, it's been about ten years since the accident." He said that he had not, but wished that he had thought about it. "Why couldn't any of this have waited until a decent hour? She told me that she just got into town, and I no more believe that any more than I do she's our mom. What do you suppose is going on right now?"

"Hang on, I'm getting a call from Toby. He's going to be pissed." When she hung up the phone, she reached out to her family to get things settled up about this. If this person really was their mother, why the fuck didn't she reach out to them all instead of using a phone? And how did she get her phone number? It wasn't the company number but her personal one that no one had but family and a few take-out places. Damn it, there were more questions than answers about this, and she wanted to hunt her down and figure this out. *"She said that she was in a coma for the last few years and that Dad lied to us."*

They had each heard from her by now, and the only one that hadn't had been Belinda. If the person really was her mother, then she'd missed out on a lot of things. Like the death of Benson and the grandchildren, Belinda moving to Ohio to start a new life, and even Toby's kids, all of them under the age of ten.

"I was just thinking about contacting dad. It's been a while, but I should be able to talk to him." Calhoun said he'd do it now, and Rogen thanked him for that. *"All right. I know that we should more than likely wait until later in the morning, but whatever this woman is up to, it's not going to go over well with anyone if she's lying."*

Calhoun didn't contact their dad with all of them on the same link. She thought that was smart of him. If she were indeed alive, then he'd be the one to get pissed off at their father rather than all of them at one time. If she were really alive, she was going to be really pissed off at both of them. There just wasn't any reason for them to be told that she was dead when she had been kicking around for some time now. At least the three months she'd told her that she was looking for them. And that, too, bothered her. Why didn't she reach out like family could do? Why do this on the phone, trying to convince them one at a time who she was to them? No reason that she could think of other than she wasn't really their mother.

Weston joined her in the office and brought her a cup of tea and some of the cookies that had been in their picnic dinner tonight. She was just munching on them when her brother contacted her again. The news wasn't good.

"Whoever she is, she's not our mother."

~*~

Danielle knew that her family had been killed in the living room. Her father had done it when he just simply couldn't take it anymore. His mother had treated him like dirt, and his grandparents didn't have the backbone to deal with her. So he'd killed both his grandparents, hating that she'd been told that he'd killed his own grandda, but he'd seen too much when he had killed his mother with an axe to the back of her head. She never cared for her grandmother—not that many people did, but she was gone now, and thankfully, she'd been the last person alive in the Pine family to inherit.

She'd not only gotten the house, a big nine-bedroom estate, but she'd gotten all the money that had been left behind as well. There was even a trust set up so that the taxes were paid each year for her, so she'd not have to worry about it. With the land surrounding the house that was rented to farmers around the area, she had a tidy income so that she'd have food in her belly when she was hungry. And it couldn't have come at a better time than it had.

About a year ago now, she'd not just lost her job but her apartment as well. The company that she'd worked for had decided that they didn't want to deal with the public anymore, and her apartment complex had decided to sell out, and the new owners were giving everyone two weeks to get their things out of their building before it was torn down. Some of her neighbors had lost everything when the bulldozers showed up on the fourteenth day and dozed all their belongings into the ground like they were nothing. She'd been living out of her car since then and had only just been notified by the family attorney to say that she had inherited the estate and everything that had gone with it.

Jameson Sheppard, a good friend of hers from college, had been very helpful to her since he'd been one of the attorneys who had been notified about the family being killed, leaving her everything. He and the family had been helpful too in getting things cleaned out of the house that she didn't want, and she was well on her way to getting the house set up just the way that she wanted it to be.

He'd also said that he was going to be looking into her losing her apartment. No one could just tell you that you had only two weeks to get out of a place, and them not offering compensation for her to find another apartment wasn't right either. She wasn't worried about that now, as she had a roof over her head, but he'd been really nice to her so far that she couldn't turn him down when he said he wanted to help her. He was a good man, she thought.

The only room that she'd been having trouble with was the master suite. It wasn't the room that was giving her trouble, but what she'd found in the room. Her grandmother had had notes in thick books about every person in town. Little snippets of information that could have been used for blackmailing them, even children. One that bothered her the most was about five-year-old Peter Day. The note said the little boy picked his nose. What reason would she have for keeping that sort of information about a child? She didn't want to know, nor did she care to find out. Grandmother wasn't the best sort of person to be around, even when you were family.

Carrie, Archie's wife, could see ghosts and had dealt with her family before they crossed over to the next place. She'd told her that her dad had sobbed about being dead and wanted to know if she could send him back for two months so that he could live a few weeks more without his mother's constant harping on him. The poor man hadn't anything else to hold him here, so he had left when Carrie had told him she couldn't do that for him. To be under such restraints, like he'd been only to be killed a few hours after he'd killed his family, would make her sad when she thought about it. Poor, poor man, her dad was.

Opening the door when her new doorbell sounded—her grandmother had had a herd of elephants running through a forest as the sound when she'd moved in—she was surprised to see Amber, Wrangler's wife, there on the stoop. Inviting her in, she said she didn't want to mess up her time there. Danielle assured her that the only thing she was doing was thinking, and that might get her into trouble.

"I know how that is. I get myself in trouble a great deal when I have nothing to occupy my time." She laughed with the other women. "The reason I'm here is that I wanted to invite you to have lunch with us tomorrow. The women in the family get together once a week when we can to have lunch and to talk about life in general."

"But I'm not part of your family." Amber waved her off, saying that she might as well be for as much as they all loved her already. "I'd love to have lunch with you and the other ladies then. I have an appointment in the morning with Jameson at the bank, but other than that, I'm free all day."

"I heard that you were going to talk to the farmers who are renting your land from you. Jameson said that since you've decided to allow them to continue renting it, he said you've made a lot of people happy." She told her that as long as they continued to pay on time, she didn't want them to leave her. "Jameson said that as well. Now that you've met all the brothers, we figured that you'd enjoy a day out with us."

"I've not. Met all the brothers yet." She cocked

her head at her when she entered the house. "Not that it matters, but I've not met Beau. He's been taking college classes, I was told, so that he could cook for himself. I think that's commendable. Maybe I'll do the same now that I have time to devote to some more college classes to learn the basics. I can't cook at all, but for a few basic things like grilled cheese and maybe some tomato soup from a can."

"He's learning how to cook so much more than that. He had Wrangler and I over for dinner the other night, and we were both impressed with his skills. You should do it." She said she was just enjoying the freedom of life right now. "I can well imagine that too. You've not had a great year from what I've heard from Jameson."

"What did you mean about me meeting all the brothers? And what does that have to do with having lunch with you guys?" She said that she'd hoped that she was one of their mates. "Mates as in wives or something? No thanks. If I had wanted a husband, I could go to any police station and find myself a man who would do that for me." Amber asked what she meant by that. "It's just that I don't want anyone to take my freedom away from me now that I have it. I've heard about mates all my life, and I want nothing to do with them."

"The Sheppard men aren't like that." She only nodded. "They aren't. I swear. They would die for their mates, and it would be something small to them. The men in this family grew up with a person worse than your grandmother and managed to turn out all right."

"I know that Jameson has, and the others seem to be really nice, but I've only just gotten things to where I don't have to work for a while, and it's all mine. To have someone come along and tell me that I have to have him run things for me just doesn't appeal to me. Thanks, but no thanks." Amber just smiled at her. "Am I still invited to lunch tomorrow? I can understand if you say no."

"We want you there. And the sooner you meet Beau, the better if he's your mate." She didn't say anything about her not meeting Beau because she was going to avoid that as much as he could. As she'd told her, she didn't want a man coming along that was going to ruin things for her when they were perfectly fine the way that they were. "I'll pick you up since I don't know where it is that we're going yet."

They made arrangements for what time she was going to pick her up, and Amber left. After closing the door, Danielle made her way to the kitchen to read the instructions again on how to microwave her lunch. The instructions were plain enough, but she didn't know what wattage her microwave was, so she was having a hard time figuring out what time she should cook it for. It had taken her fifteen minutes of reading the manual that had come with it when she bought it to know how to set up the power settings. Putting it in the thing, she decided to watch it carefully to make sure she didn't burn it like she had her supper last evening. She'd gotten distracted and had forgotten about it until it was too late. And she wasn't going to think about the burnt popcorn that she'd decided to have after the meal disaster.

She'd done all right for herself this time and was eating her lunch when the front doorbell rang again. Going to the door, she was surprised to see Jameson there with one of his brothers. She just knew that it was going to be Beau and that Amber had sent him here so that she could test the theory about him being her mate.

"I'm staying right here, and you two are going to go home." Jameson laughed and told her that he had been sent by Carrie, the leap bitch. "I don't care what she is, I've decided to not have a mate, and while the idea is probably nothing I can do anything about, I'm not going to allow you anywhere near me."

"Sounds like a plan that I can get behind. However, I don't have a choice in the matter. I have to make sure." She simply stepped back into her house and closed the door behind her. There was no way she was going to allow anyone to do anything with her new life without a fight. The doorbell rang again. When she opened the door, it was Beau at the door, and it was too late for her to do anything when he touched his hand to her arm. "I'm sorry."

Leaping back from him, she was surprised when he moved when she did. Had he not been there for her, she would have fallen to the floor, down the stairs that led to the doorway, and busted her head. All she could do was look up at him when he held her in his arms.

"Well?" He only had to nod when she asked if she was his mate or not. "Great. Just what I needed. I don't suppose you'll give me a month to get used to living here by myself, will you? I've only just moved in and I haven't even had my first meal in the house."

"I heard what you think of having a mate, and you can take all the time you need." She asked him if he was always a bastard. "I don't think I'm being one now. I belong to you, and you tell me when it is that you want me to be a part of the life that you've carved out for yourself. I don't have a house as yet, so I couldn't tell you how you feel about owning your first home."

"I've heard that you won't make me do anything that I don't want to do, but I'm having a hard time believing it after all the mates I've seen together." He said that he wouldn't dare make her do a thing that she didn't want to do. "I guess time will tell. Now that you've worked your way into my house and life."

Chapter 2

Beau had taken all the classes that had been offered at the college for basic cooking. He felt really good about being able to feed himself and his mate if she were to come around. And now that she did, she was upset with him for being pushy. He'd have to talk to his brother Archie about making him go and find out. It wasn't any of his business when or if he found her, and to make him go see her wasn't right.

He thought about his mother then. How her plan had been to kill off the mates of him and his brothers so that they'd not make her a grandmother. Then, when Nash had met his mate in Sunny, a waitress from a little diner, she pitted the two of them against one another as she'd done making the brothers hate one another. It had taken a great deal of sneaking around and talking to one another to figure out her plan. Then, after that, it had gone downhill for her and her dad when the six of them had been on the same side and working against her.

It wasn't a thought that he thought about often. Had she been able to kill off any of them? They'd asked her and she had said no, but she'd been lying to them since they were children, and they didn't trust her at all. She'd even killed off their dad and grandmother when they got in the way of what she was doing. But she was dead now, along with her dad, and they had been living the life that they thought they deserved. Now he had a mate, and he wasn't sure what to think about that.

He'd heard about Danielle, of course. She'd been living in the Pine mansion since coming to town after the family had been murdered. He'd not had the opportunity to meet her as he'd been really busy with classes, but now that he had, he didn't know how to convince her that he wasn't going to make her do anything. Just the opposite, he thought, in that he'd wait for her direction on how things were to go.

He was standing in the middle of his nearly empty apartment when he realized that he'd not need the house that he'd been planning on building, nor the land that was part of the estate that their father had left them. While he didn't think that it would matter what he did with the land, he wasn't going to do anything that might piss off Danielle in the meantime. She was doing that already, and he didn't want to add to her day.

When his cell phone rang with just a number, he answered it so that he could hang up again if it was someone that he didn't want to talk to. When no one said anything, he was nearly ready to hang up when he heard someone sobbing. Waiting for the person to tell him what was going on, he went out of his place to get to his car faster if they needed him somewhere.

"What did you do?" He asked the woman to repeat herself. "It's Danielle Pine. I thought I told you that I didn't want anything to do with you. So what did you do about sending faeries around here to help me? And I'm using that term lightly as they're driving me crazy right now. So again, what did you do?"

"Nothing. I swear it." She told him that there were about a thousand little people in her house right now that were helping her get things squared away. "I don't even know what that might mean, but I didn't have anything to do with them coming to your home. I have a few dozen in my apartment now, but I didn't send—I didn't even tell anyone that you're my mate."

"I asked about that, and they told me that the magic surrounding you told them. Now I have magic too, they're telling me." He said that he'd not directed any kind of magic to her. "Well, are you coming over here to take care of this? I don't know what I'm supposed to do with them around here all the time. There are just too many of them—can you just get here soon and tell them that I don't need them? I don't want to hurt their feelings again. When I tried to get them to go away, I could feel their hurt. I can't handle that or them. Come and take them back with you."

"I'll come over, but I don't know what you

expect me to do with them all now that they've found out about you. I didn't even tell my brother Archie and his wife, Sunny. Sunny is the daughter of the boss of the faeries, so I'm not sure—"

"You have to come here and straighten this out. I don't know Sunny well enough to know her mother yet, but I'm thinking that she found out somehow, or they might well have magic that tells them how this happened." She sobbed again. "All I wanted to do was microwave my dinner tonight after taking a long nap. Now I'm stressed out and can't think right. And it's all your fault. I told you this would happen. Now my life is messed up. Because of you."

"I'm sorry. But I didn't have anything to do— you know what? I'm on my way. I'll figure out how they found out about us, and I'll make sure they know that you don't need them." She told him not to hurt their feelings. "I'll try not to do that, but I can't promise anything about that. I've not had to deal with them much, so I'm not sure how to get them to cooperate. All right? I'm on my way there now."

He didn't have a clue how he was supposed to not hurt their feelings. He'd been truthful about telling her that he'd not dealt with them all that much, so he didn't know how to not hurt their feelings. Getting in his car, he was nearly there when what he was doing occurred to him. Pulling off to the side of the road, he laughed until he hurt. He didn't even know how she'd gotten his number, but was dropping everything that he had planned for the day to help her with a faerie problem.

He didn't even get a chance to ring the doorbell when the door was opened, and he was pulled into the house. When he saw just how many faeries were in the front hallway, he took a step back from them. There had to be at least a couple of thousand of them in the main hallway.

"Hello, Master Beau. My name is Honey. This is Stack. We're in charge of the faeries." When Danielle said that she knew who they were, they fluttered to him and landed on his outstretched hand. "We have stressed the young miss out. It wasn't our intention when we came here. Our only intention was to help her clean the manor up. There are still blood stains on the floor in the front room."

"I told them I was going to put a carpet over it, but they insisted that it needed to be cleaned up." She'd been crying, and his heart hurt for that. He looked at Honey and asked why there were so many of them here. "That's something that I'd like to know as well."

"This house is a manor that hasn't been touched in decades, and with all of us willing to work for her, we thought it would take us less time to get it cleaned up, and she'd not have to worry with it." Beau pointed out that was how they'd stressed her out. "I understand that now, Master Beau. It wasn't what we wanted when we came here."

"Perhaps you can tell us why you're here and who sent you?" Honey said that they'd been living around here for decades, but were not able to do anything with the gardens that came with the house. "There are gardens here?"

One look at Danielle and he had to hide a smile. She apparently didn't know about any gardens either. So, for some reason, that had him laughing quietly. He'd never laugh at her out loud as she was already stressed out enough to cause tears, so he looked at Honey again, asking him why they were so quick to want to start on the gardens.

"They used to be, at one time, the glory of this house. The house sang with happiness, too, when the flowers were in bloom. But for the last fifty or so years, the gardens have been left to ruin, and we wanted to bring them back to life. You've been told that children have the best sort of magic." He said that he had been told that at some point in his life. "There are flowers and plants growing here that grow nowhere else around here. With the house being cleaned, we thought perhaps she'd allow us to go to the gardens and bring it back too."

"Why didn't you tell me that?" He thought it was a good question and decided to allow Honey or Stack to answer. It was Stack that answered Danielle. "Oh. I understand now. I should have allowed you to speak instead of yelling at you when you got here. That's all on me. But one of you could have interrupted me and told me what was going on."

"We were trying hard not to stress you out." Beau couldn't help it then; he laughed. "She's been very stressed out for a few days now. We wanted to unburden her by making sure that the house is in tiptop shape for you and her. You will be living here, correct, Master Beau?"

"We're still working things out." He thought that was a good answer and was glad that Danielle didn't say anything differently about their living arrangements. Instead, she told Honey that they could do the gardens and house, but not to stress her out more. "I'm assuming that you'll all not be staying here when this is finished?"

"You wish us to leave?" The sound of his breaking heart was heard by him, and apparently, Danielle too. She was quick to tell them that they'd have to work that out as well as they were only just getting to know one another. "'Tis a large home, my lady, and it will take a pip of us to keep up with it. Right now, there is a need for a new furnace as this one is already broken, and you have several leaks in the roof that need to be repaired before they do much more damage to the ceiling in the upper floors."

"How much will it cost me to have those things fixed. I have money, but not a lot of disposable income right now." Stack said that they could have it repaired in no time with no cost to her. "You can't just fix it without some help from someone bigger, can you? I mean, I don't know anything about furnaces, but I know it's a big job."

"We have magic." That didn't sound like a good reason for them to be fixing the furnace, but he didn't comment when Danielle didn't. "We can do anything that you need done to the house. Such as filling the rooms out that are now empty. We'll just adjust things to suit you as you wish."

"You mean you can put furniture in the rooms that are empty without me having to go to the store to buy them? I don't know about that. Isn't that going to put someone out of business? I'd hate to be a part of someone going out of business because I had some faeries that could magically make things for me." He loved the way that she was thinking, but that had nothing to do with why there were so many of them here. "Look. You can fix up my house, but repairs that are going to be costly need to be cleared by me. You can fix the furnace and roof because I don't even want to begin on trying to get those fixed right now, but the rest we'll work out as we go." He asked about the gardens. "Don't let anyone notice you so that you don't get into trouble with your boss or Sunny, but you can fix them up, too. I'd love to see what the gardens look like when they're not a bunch of weeds taking up the entire back yard."

After Honey and Stack went to the rest of the pip—he'd only just figured out that a pip was a bunch of faeries—he turned to look at Danielle. She looked no less stressed, but he could tell she was embarrassed, too. He asked her what was going on.

"Everything. Did you know what they wanted before they got here?" He told her that he'd not only that she was sounding stressed, and he wanted to help her out. "Thank you for that. Especially after I treated you like shit earlier. When I called Jameson, he told me to call you and gave me your number so that I could. I don't remember why he thought it was a good idea to call you instead of him helping me, but he said you'd get to the bottom of it, and I guess you did."

"Are you all right now? You still look like you're stressed out." She told him what her plan had been when they showed up. "You must be getting sick of sandwiches. I know that if I had to eat them all the time, I would be."

"I don't know how to cook. Not anything. I burnt a bag of popcorn last night and had to leave the windows open all night to get the smell out of the house. My new microwave is probably permanently going to smell like it for the rest of its life." He told her that the faeries would probably take care of it for her. "Yeah, I guess they could. They're already going to fix my furnace. I had no idea that those things were wrong with this house when I moved in. I wonder what else is wrong with it. I'm sure, as how tight my grandmother was with money and knowing that the furnace was broken long before they died, I can't imagine that too many things got fixed when they were broken."

"Doubtful. I knew your grandmother; she wasn't anyone that I would have hung out with even on her best days." She said that she could understand that. And she was related to her. "I'm profoundly sorry for that. And for the loss of your dad. He was a good man when he was out from under her control. Which wasn't all that often."

"I didn't know him all that well. When it became unbearable for me to come here and visit him, I stopped coming. He didn't put up a fuss about me not coming around. I always had the feeling that, for as much as she was mean to me, she was ten times worse to him when I left. But he saved everything that I sent him over the years for his birthday and Christmas."

"That was good of him." He looked around the room he was in and told her that he'd never been in the house before. "I mean, I knew who lived here, but I didn't bother with coming around. She and my mother could have been cut from the same cloth; they were so mean to everyone else. I have a feeling that they would have been best friends."

"I've heard about your mom and her dad. They were quite the pair, weren't they?" He said that she had

no idea. "I probably don't want to know either. But if
you need a reason to bitch about them, you can come
over and we can talk about them. I'm sorry for the way
that I treated you this morning. I wasn't having a good
day."

"Understandable." He asked if she was all right
now. "I think you just needed them to listen to you, and
it could have all been cleared up. Or you're listening to
them. I'm not sure what the breakdown was."

"They made me nervous, there were so many of
them." He said that he'd gotten the same overwhelming
feeling, too, when he'd come to the house. "So I was
right in thinking that there were so many of them.
How many do you have in your apartment? You do
live in one, I was told, correct?"

"Yes, I have an apartment. I was going to build
on the land that my father left me, but I've decided to
put that off for now." She asked him if it was because
she had a house already. "Yes, that's part of it. I don't
know that you'd want to live anywhere else but here.
I'll live where you are if we ever get to that point." She
changed the subject as soon as he finished talking.

"I'd invite you to dinner, but all I'm having is
half of a sub. The rest will be my dinner tomorrow
night after I have lunch with the women tomorrow."
He asked if she'd mind if he cooked for her. "That
would be fantastic, but I don't have anything to cook
with. All the pots and pans that were here before I

moved in have been thrown out. They were old and worn to nothing anyway."

"Come to my place and I'll feed you. I have everything I need to make some good tomato sauce and pasta. I was at the top of my class when it came to making noodles. I find that I love making them whenever I can." She said that she didn't know what homemade anything tasted like. "Of course you don't. We're just getting to know one another right now without the faeries being a distraction."

"Thank you." He was excited to have her come to his place. There was a great deal going on at her home at the present time, and he wanted to show her how he could cook. It was small in comparison to what she would bring to them as a couple, but cooking would relax him, and, in turn, hopefully relax her as well. It's all he wanted right now was to make her feel better about life in general.

~*~

Danielle didn't know what to expect, but the state of his home wasn't it. There wasn't much in the way of furniture and even less in things that reflected the man that she was slowly beginning to know. While not at all messy, it had nothing much more than the basic needs in the house that he lived in.

A couch that had seen better days, perhaps years ago. His kitchen had a card table in it with three mismatched chairs. In the dish drainer, there were five plates and some silverware that looked as mismatched as his chairs had. Upon arriving, he showed her where the bathroom was and told her that he'd only just had it cleaned, and the towels were also cleaned up. They didn't match one another either, and she thought that was really sad.

To be as rich as she'd heard that he was and have nothing to show for it made her heart hurt for him. It all had to do with his mother; she just knew it. She must have been a cruel task maker, as she'd heard she'd been. Not allowing them any freedom when they had moved out of her home, where that should have been the end of it.

Watching him pull out what he called a pasta maker, she wanted to sit in the kitchen area and watch him make them. After putting a great deal of flour on the counter, he cracked some eggs in the center and began mixing the ingredients together. When the dough was made, he said it had to 'rest' while he had to make the sauce.

"In some parts of the states, they call the sauce gravy. Since I love gravy and mashed potatoes, I've never been keen on calling it that." He chopped up some tomatoes with some of the green leafy plants he had on the counter and made the entire apartment smell amazing. Watching him cook made her jealous that she couldn't get the same smells out of whatever she'd been cooking at home. "I have some loaves of bread, too, that I can make garlic toast."

By the time he was cooking the pasta for the sauce, she was starving. The smells alone were enough to have her salivating, and she'd not eaten one bite of food yet. As soon as he was dishing up their dinner, she wanted to knock him away and eat the entire pot full of pasta and sauce all on her own. It was that great.

Sitting down to eat, she no longer noticed the mismatched chairs nor the chipped plates. Dinner and the person she was having it with made her realize that it mattered little when there was good food and good company. And he was too. After giving her a small glass of wine, all she wanted they ate dinner. Danielle's first bite had her moaning at the flavors that seemed to explode in her mouth.

After they both had two helpings of the dinner, she was stuffed. The bread had been so delicious, too, that she had eaten far more than she should have. After their plates were shoved away, it was all she could do to stay awake; the carbs were hitting her hard after not getting her nap today.

"I've been really stressed out for the last couple of weeks. I thought that having my own place and money enough to afford not to work would be just what I needed to get on with my life. But I'm finding homeownership is a lot more stressful than I thought it would be." He asked her if he could help her with the house. "I think that once I get used to the faeries being around, I won't stress about the yard. I found several notices about the lawn needing to be taken care of in some of the paperwork that I found on a desk in my grandmother's room."

"I'd be more than happy to help you with anything you need." She told him that right now, she just needed to rest and then get a job. "I have to find myself one too. I've been sort of lazy about working since I was going to college. Now that I've finished up, I need to get into gear and start earning a living. I can afford not to work, for now anyway — you understand that, but I need to have something to do or I'll get myself into trouble. I have a feeling that you're the same way."

"Not so much trouble as I get bored. I was really busy when I first started on the house, tossing things out that were broken or old. Going through their things was heartbreaking, too. But since I didn't know any of them all that well, it wasn't so difficult to toss out their personal things. Except for my dad's things. That was a bit harder to go through." He asked if she was finished moving things out. "I am for the most part. The first time I went through the house, it was sort of a purge. The next time I'm going to go through the house, I'll be more selective about what I toss out. Mostly, as I said, it was broken or old stuff that had long since outlived its usefulness."

"And now you'll have the gardens finished too.

I can talk to my brother Weston about the notices if you wish. I doubt very much he's gotten that far into his job to notice if yards are mowed or not. He's doing a really great job if you were to ask me about it." She said that he might be slightly one-sided in his opinion. "True. He is my big brother after all."

They didn't go to the living room to sit and talk, but did sit at the kitchen table. When it was apparent that they were getting along well, she suggested that since he had cooked, she should do the clean-up. Beau told her that the faeries would do the cleaning up as he'd made them happy by making a mess for them.

"They thrive on helping out. Something that you're going to have to learn about them is that they had no concept of size. Since everything is bigger than they are, they just assume that when you want something, it has to be the biggest they can make." She was confused about that. "You do know that they can make things for you, don't you? They're going to be all right in fixing the furnace and roof, as they have sizes already made up for them. But if you were to tell them you needed a greenhouse, for instance, you'd have to tell them what size you want. Like lots of details in how big you want it to be. Or it might be bigger than your home that you live in now."

"I didn't know they could make things. I guess I should have when they said they could fill out the rooms for me." She sat up straighter in her chair and thought about what he was saying. "So they're not going to repair the furnace, but put in a new one that is magical. Same with the roof."

"You might not even see a difference in your old furnace and the new furnace, but it'll be magical, as you said. It will never have to be replaced. Ever. Same with the roof. It will never leak again, not even if you lose some of the roofing in a storm." She laughed, knowing that he was telling her the truth but still disbelieving of it too. How could they make it work without a big person there to show them how it would work? She didn't know and decided that she wasn't going to question their work from now on. If they fixed it, she was in good hands, she thought.

Danielle hated that Beau was going to have to take her home. But it was raining again, and she didn't drive to his house. As soon as she was at her house, she realized that she didn't want to go in and be alone. Looking at Beau, she made a decision that would affect the rest of her life, hopefully in a good way.

"Would you like to stay here with me? I'm not ready for us to be a couple, but since it will happen sooner or later, you might as well get used to the house and the things that are here." He asked her if she was sure. "Yes. I don't want to be alone either. I don't know why, but I might even sleep better if there was someone else around when I went to bed. I'm sure that the faeries would be good company, but there are just too many of them around for me to get used to them right away."

"All right. I can have the faeries make me up a room, if that's okay with you?" She said that was a brilliant idea, as she was still sleeping on the air mattress she'd brought with her when she'd moved in. "You should have them make you up a room. The master suite. If there is one. I'm assuming that there are a few bathrooms in the place."

"Not as many as there should be. There is one on each floor, and they're not close to the bedroom that I'm using. I should think about that too. Having them put in a couple more bathrooms in the place." He said he'd be happy to tell them when to begin and, with her help, where to put them. "I was thinking that each bedroom needs to have its own bathroom, but I'm not sure how that would work. Maybe I'm getting too greedy or something with them around."

"I don't know. I've never been much further in the house than the front hallway. But if that's what you want, they'll be more than happy to make you happy. I think that's what they live for, making people happy." She said she'd give it some thought. "If I'm going to stay here, I'm going to need some things from home. Tooth brush and some clean clothing."

"You go and get them, and I'll see what they've done to the house. I might have to stay with you if the house is in worse shape than it was before. I know that when I'm cleaning, that's the way things look." She was laughing when she got out of his car. "I'll see you when you return. Just be careful driving in this mess."

Danielle was giddy when she walked into her home. She was excited, too, about what she'd see. The first thing she noticed was the living room. Not only were the blood stains gone, but the whole room looked renewed and refreshed. She could get used to this.

Chapter 3

Calhoun had the information that they needed about the woman claiming to be their mother. Dad was on his way home from Europe with his new wife and said that he knew that their mother was dead; he'd seen her body. Whatever was going on, none of them could figure it out right now. Only that someone was pretending to be Marsha Watson, the long-lost mother to the six of them.

As they sat around her dining room table, Rogen was taking notes. It had been a habit that she'd picked up when talking to clients, and she'd never broken the habit as yet. Once they were all ready to talk, she told them that she'd discovered two things about this Marsha person.

"I don't think she's a shifter. I don't know why, but I have a feeling that this woman, whoever she is, has no idea that we're cats." It was her brother Tommy who asked how she could be so sure. "She didn't reach out to any of us through our family link. That would have been the most logical thing to do when she'd been trying to get in touch with us. And it's not like we put it out there that we're jaguars either. Someone who would know us would know that right away."

"Okay, that makes sense for how you put it. I agree. Either she doesn't know or hasn't figured it out that we're cats that she should be able to talk to us. Anyone else think that could be true?" They all agreed with her, and Calhoun wrote it on the side of things that they thought were true. The other side of the board was things that they did know, and there was very little on that side of the wipe-off board. "Before we get to number two on Rogen's list, I got copies of her death certificate. Also, I have copies of the insurance policies that were cashed out when she passed away. I don't know how helpful they'll be, but I thought it was better to be safe than sorry."

"I agree with you on that. This whole thing makes me nervous." Belinda said that she was more pissed off than nervous about this. To think that she'd been buried over ten years ago and was just now coming around pissed her off. Rogen nodded as she continued. "The second thing is something that I've only been tossing around. It's to do with my being married to the Sheppard's family. We all have money right now, and anyone in the world could find out about the Sheppards having money. I think that it's just too convenient for this to be happening right now when we're all together and making a good living for ourselves."

"I actually thought of that too." Tommy looked

around the table as he continued to speak. "None of us is hurting for money right now, and it's only been for the last few years that we can all say that. Even Belinda is doing well with her job and not having to pay extra fines for her leap."

Belinda, her sister-in-law, had been paying dues to Weston as the leap leader and fines to her old leap leader, too. He was pocketing the money that he collected from a great many people that way, and when the king of their kind found out, he fired him for his dirty dealings. In turn, since Belinda had been the one who had told him about the double fines, Weston had given her a bonus in the money that he'd collected that month, and it made her very happy.

"So you think that she's out to get money from us? How do you suppose that's going to work when none of us believe that she's our mother?" It was Calhoun who suggested blackmail. "Okay, perhaps I can understand that better if you were to let me know how you think she's going to be able to do that."

"We cashed the insurance when she died to pay for the funeral. It was the only way that it would have been paid for; if we hadn't done that, we'd still be paying it off." Sandy said she thought that was a lame excuse to blackmail someone. "Do you have a better idea? It's the only reason that I can think of for her to be coming around and trying to contact us. Even Dad thinks that she's here to get money from us."

"I can understand why she'd wait until now to come after us. Like you said, we all have money now. But I don't understand why she'd think she was going to get away with it. I've not seen a picture of our mom since the funeral. Do you suppose she's been waiting all this time because she's had work done on her face? That would take a lot of preplanning, and her not knowing about the money that we have now. Ten years ago, we didn't any of us have a pot to piss in. And she would have known it. In all that time, too, we've had some terrible things happen. Did she ask any of you what happened to Benson and his two kids? And why she couldn't get in touch with them?"

"I never thought of that." Most of the table hadn't thought of it, and Rogen felt bad because it made Belinda sad for a moment.

Danny, Sandy's ex-husband, had murdered Benson and their two children for the insurance that he'd taken out on them. After cleaning out her house after divorcing him, she'd found more policies with names of people who were elderly down her street and the rest of the family, including her. He had planned on killing them all off for a nice payday. The fucking bastard was now in prison where he belonged. Where he should have been decades ago.

It was mind-boggling to think that after all this time, their mother had decided to show up and want something from them. Of course, they didn't know that for sure, but there was no other reason for her to contact them now after being presumed dead after all this time.

Their mother hadn't been a terrible person, not like some of the parents that she'd met through her work. But she did drink a great deal. That was what had caused the accident, they'd found out. Their mother had been very drunk when she had an accident with the car that she had been driving. Rogen had never understood that part, as their mother was a shifter too, and it would take a great deal of alcohol to get her intoxicated enough to be considered drunk. But it had happened, and she had died, so they didn't look into it too deeply.

"Dad's plane just landed. He said that the car you had there for him has picked him up, and he's on his way here. He, too, has a death certificate as well as the paperwork from the autopsy that was performed after her death. I would think that that's a good indication that she was killed that night." Rogen got up to have the staff bring in drinks and snacks. She never dreamed that they'd be talking about this right now and wanted to get it over with and find out what the hell was going on.

No one had heard from their mother since the night she called them all at three in the morning, telling them that she'd only just gotten out of a coma and she'd been looking for them. Also, apparently, she'd only just gotten into town. Whether that was the town they now lived in or the town they'd come from, no one knew, but it was something that they were looking for answers about.

"I've checked with the hotels around the town. None of them has a Marsha Watson in their groups. The bed and breakfast doesn't have anyone by that name either. Unless she's changed her name for some reason." Sandy asked about the hotels where they used to live. "Most of them said no, they didn't have her on their books, but a lot of them said they couldn't tell me because of privacy rules regarding her stay."

"This is just stupid." She couldn't agree more with her brother on that. "I'm actually losing sleep over this nightmare because we buried the wrong person, or worse, she really has been in a coma and we're all guilty of not believing her."

"What else are we supposed to do right now? I mean, none of us has a way to contact her. Unless any of you have tried to reach out to her? Have you?" No one had, but they had thought about it. "Wouldn't that be the best way to figure this out? To see if she's really out there and we are going crazy over nothing?"

Calhoun said he'd do it now. As they waited for him to tell them if it worked or not, she did the same thing and reached out to their dad. She wanted him to know that she had a place for him to stay and that he was welcome there for as long as he wished. He was happy sounding when he answered her.

"I've not seen any of you for so long, I nearly forgot what it's like to have you all together. How is everyone doing?" She knew that he knew about Benson being killed with his two grandchildren. She'd also updated him on the fact that Danny had done it to them. She would reach out to him on his birthday and the holidays and update him on the goings on with the family. *"I don't want to put you out when you're only just newly married, Rogen. How about I stay in a hotel until we can get this figured out?"*

"You came alone?" He said that Mildred had had some work to do, and she wouldn't know anyone anyway. *"But she won't get to know us if she doesn't come around, Dad. You should have made her come with you so that we could all be together for a change."*

"I tried, but she said that she didn't want to come out, so I left her at home to work. She said that she gets more done without me being around anyway." Dad changed the subject. *"Are the grandkids going to be around, too? I've missed most of their lives, and I'm looking forward to meeting them."*

She told him how they all lived around one another and how they got together every week so that they could all catch up on things. Even though they were all together, it would be days before they would actually be able to have a conversation with each other.

"We usually meet at my house and go over things

that have happened in the week. They bring the kids, too."
He said that he was looking forward to seeing everyone
and getting to know the kids. *"They're all here now. The
kids are playing in the back yard as the weather has turned
really nice after raining all day yesterday."*

"The weather is always nice where I live." They
talked about his plans of staying for a week or longer,
depending on when they could get this all taken care
of. *"I never dreamed that this would happen. We buried her,
and I thought that was about as final as it could be."*

*"I know, Dad. We've been talking about it too.
Calhoun is reaching out to her now, but he's not telling
us whether or not he's gotten in touch with her. It's been
a nightmare around here with all the things that are going
on."* He told her to keep her chin up, something that he
said to them all at some point in their lives. *"I'm going
to be there in forty minutes I was told. You keep them there
so that I can see them. I might be a little teary-eyed from
missing so much, but we'll be together again, and that's all a
man can hope for when it comes to his family."*

After closing the connection, she looked
around at her family. They were all currently staring
at Calhoun to see if he was getting through to their
mother or not, but she'd bet that he wasn't having any
luck, just by the look on his face. When he shook his
head and looked so sad, she wanted to hunt down this
person who said they were their mother and beat the
shit out of her. This was no way to treat strangers who

were still grieving the loss of their parent.

"Nothing. It was as if I was reaching out to the air and there was no one there to answer me." Rogen asked him what he thought that meant, not sure if it could mean that the woman was lying. "I think it's just as we said, she hasn't any idea that we're shifters and never planned on that being brought up."

"I'm not saying I believe that she's our mom or not, but could the link be messed up because it's not been used in a decade? I might be grasping at straws right now, but I don't think I can take any more disappointment concerning the losses we've experienced. Not just Benson and the kids, but with dad moving away and never coming back. With this crap with Danny and him trying to kill the rest of us for money. I would like for one thing to go right for a change. Wouldn't you guys?"

"Yes, I would." She pulled tissues from the box that was on the table, along with the snacks and drinks. After blowing her nose, she looked at each of their faces. "I don't know if I could have survived this without you guys around. And I know that at least a couple of you feel the same way."

They all did. Once the tissue box made its round around the table, she laughed a little. "Weston is going to come home and wonder what we've been up to if we don't stop crying. I have cried a river thinking about all the what-ifs or how-comes. If we could just talk to her again to see what the hell she wants from us, I'd feel a good deal better. The not knowing is driving me crazy. I don't know about you guys, but I just want this to be taken care of so that we can move on with our lives."

Calhoun, being the oldest, said that he had lost a great many nights of rest from this, and it turned out that all of them had. She knew that she was sleeping worse than she had when she had a large project coming up. There wasn't enough information for them to make a solid plan for when or if she showed up. Some kind of indication about her plans would make them all a little less stressed about any and all of this.

~*~

Beau loved the old house. Some things needed to be taken care of. The kitchen was outdated and needed new appliances. He'd bet anything that it hadn't been updated since the forties, if not longer. The refrigerator didn't work anymore, and that was one of the things she was going to have replaced from a store. There were coolers all around the room that made him think that the sucker had been out for some time, and they were simply making do with what they had on hand. Then there was the stove. He wouldn't use it even if he was starving to death, and that was the only way to cook something. It was so outdated that he was fearful of it blowing up the house when the gas was turned on. Tomorrow, both appliances were going to be delivered. Also, he looked at the dining room and was appalled.

He knew that Danielle had been eating in the big room, but it looked to him like the place hadn't had a good cleaning for decades. The faeries had gotten on it when he mentioned that it needed to be cleaned. Right now, after they were finished, it still needed a new table and chairs, as the ones that were in the room looked like they'd been through a war zone or something. There were scratches in the table top, and it looked as if the legs had been chewed on by a dog or something else he didn't want to think about. There had been so much dust on the table that he didn't know it was a dark wood until it was cleaned up.

The bedrooms that hadn't been used were in better shape than the rest of the house. They were dirty and needed the windows cleaned. But once the faeries were finished with them, they did shine up really nicely. The only rooms that were taking the longest to clean were the master suite that her grandmother had taken over when she'd moved in, as well as the bedroom for the great grandparents. The room was much too small for two people, much less a bed and furniture. All of the furniture was going out on the next purge, she told him. She'd left the rooms that they occupied alone in favor of cleaning them out first and then deciding what she wanted to do with them.

Her father's bedroom told of a man who was used to having discipline. The room and the furniture were all old and musty-smelling, but it was neat as a pen, and even his shoes had been lined up on the floor of the closet. His things would also be going out with the next time she was ready to get rid of the stuff in the house that she no longer thought she could use.

"I've had the faeries redo the master bedroom. I have no idea why, but I think we'll need a bigger bed than the one that was in there. You're a large man, and I don't want to be crowded in a room with stuff that belongs to us both." He told her that he'd take care of that. "Good. Also, since the kitchen needs to be updated too, I was thinking that we could go out to dinner tonight and have some fun. All we've been doing is fretting over this house for so long that I'm sick of it. What do you say?"

"I say that's a wonderful idea." She nodded, but he could tell she had more on her mind than just dinner. "Is there anything I can do to help you out? You seem really stressed right now."

"I'm going to have them fix up the bathrooms the way that we talked about it. The master looks so much better enlarged, and with the double bathroom in there, we'll have plenty of room to get dressed in the morning." He said that he'd noticed too that there wasn't any carpet in the room. "Yes, it was nasty in there, I noticed, and then I figured that we'd be better off with hardwood floors rather than a carpet that needs to be vacuumed every day. At least with hardwood floors, they can be dusted instead of swept up."

There was more to it, so when she walked away, he let her. She would come to him later and tell him what she'd been thinking, but for now she needed to think things through and figure them out. He loved that she didn't need to empty her head when she had something to say; she'd say it. But only after she'd worked it out a great deal in her mind.

The house was coming along nicely. Having the faeries cleaning the rooms was working out better than they thought it would. It also made it so that she could figure out what she wanted done with each room. The living room was the only room that was completed, and it looked like a dream. Instead of just cleaning the room, she'd had them clean the wallpaper as well as the fireplace, too, so that they could enjoy the room better. He loved the old-fashioned wallpaper in the room and didn't mind at all that it was from a different era. While this was going on, the garden was being taken care of.

He'd been outside just yesterday to see the progress they were making. By then, they'd had the tall weeds taken down and some of the fixtures that were out there—a large fountain was in the middle of the tall grass and weeds, along with several topiaries around the garden that needed to be repaid. They were taking their time with the area, so they didn't mess with the long-dormant flowers and roses around the fountain and other planters.

There was also an herb garden right off the kitchen that they were going to bring back for him to use in his cooking. He loved cooking with fresh when he could get it. And from the size of the garden, he was going to be able to cook anything that he wanted and use the fresh herbs out there.

When Danielle found him on the second floor, where the bedrooms were that they weren't using, she asked him if there was a certain room that he wanted all for himself. Asking her what she meant, she mentioned the office and how it was on her list of things to get organized.

"You're still going through the things that were left behind, right?" She told him that she was nearly finished in there if he wanted to go have a look at it. "You've been using the paper shredder, correct? I'd hate for some of that to get in the wrong hands at this late date."

"I've shredded everything that was paper. Even if I couldn't find any information on it, I wasn't going to take any chances." He smiled at her. "I'm going to need to get another trash can from the trash company if we keep purging things out of here. I never realized how time-consuming this was going to be when I started. But I have to admit, I'm having fun doing it. It's like I'm renewing the house from what it had been. A junk pile."

"Yes, I have to agree with you on that. It has been a junk pile of things. I'm just glad we have the faeries to help us out, or there is no telling what we'd have to do to get this place in shape." She nodded and looked around the room he was in. "I was thinking that I'd take this room since it seems to be bigger than the others."

"I'm still sleeping in the living room for now. I want the master suite to be just for us. No one else will sleep in there but the two of us when we get to that point in our relationship." He loved it when she talked like that. It made it seem like she was thinking about the two of them as a couple and not someone who was just staying with her while she got the house under control. "I suppose that I could sleep in one of the other bedrooms that are finished, but I've not had the energy to go up to bed yet, much less try and blow up the mattress again."

They both laughed. There was a bed in each of the rooms that the faeries had put in there for them. The empty bedrooms were finished as well, but for the bed, there was nothing at all in the room as yet. He knew they'd need a dresser or two, but they were focusing their time on the rest of the house for now and would get to that part later.

"I'll help you with your mattress. The one that I've been sleeping on is really nice. You should take the next bedroom so that you'll get off the floor." She said that she was thinking that very same thing. "Good. I hate using a bed when you're still using the air mattress in the front room."

They were getting along well, he thought. They talked most evenings about everything that they were doing to the house. Then, in the morning, over toast and tea, they would gather up the faeries that were still working in the house and tell them what they were planning. Most of the time, they'd be very helpful, but there were times when they'd be in the way more than not. But they loved having them around, and they were a great help when it came to getting the rooms up to par, like they wanted them to be.

"Mistress, we have a surprise for you." She looked like she didn't want another surprise, but told them to tell her what they'd done. "Come see the kitchen. We have been taking ideas from the master, as he knows how to cook, and have come up with a good idea of what he wanted in the room."

"You remember that the stove and refrigerator are going to be delivered tomorrow, correct? You didn't put on in the places that we discussed, did you?" He assured her that the kitchen would be ready for the two things now. "I thank you for doing this for us. You guys are working so hard that I feel bad when you do something like the kitchen for us."

"It is our pleasure to make you happy." He'd told Danielle that before. They lived to make the people that they worked for happy. "We think that you'll both love the kitchen now that it's finished."

Walking into the large room, he nearly fell over when he got a look at the room. It was finished, and it looked like a cook's dream. The countertops were beautifully laid and looked so nice with the new splashboard above them. There was a sink that was large enough to put pots in to be cleaned, and a faucet over the stove to fill pots when needed.

He could see himself cooking all kinds of meals in this room and never tiring of it. The way that it looked right now had him wanting to fill it up with scents from the garden and eat right on the beautiful small table when it was finished. He looked at Danielle to judge her take on the room.

"It's beautiful and makes me want to learn to cook." Beau laughed, and it felt good. He looked at the smaller appliances that were scattered around the countertops and went to see what they were. "Did you see the tea maker? We can have fresh tea made daily for us when we want. I love this room."

They talked about the different things that the room had. There was a pantry just off the main area that would hold a plethora of things that they might need. Also, he noticed a washer and dryer had been put in the space for cleaning the kitchen things when they were dirty. The spaces for the fridge and stove were spotless and looked ready to be hooked up to the new ones coming tomorrow. He couldn't believe how much room he had in the room that he was going to use as much as he could. The heavy-duty mixer was going to be perfect for making bread and pasta. There was a microwave that looked large enough to cook a turkey in. They marveled at the dishes that were in the cabinets for everyday use. He even loved the double dishwasher so that when his family came over to eat with them, there would be plenty of room to get the dishes cleaned up without someone having to hand-wash them all.

"You do like the room, do you not?" They both answered at the same time and said yes, they did. The room was spectacular. And just the way that they wanted it. "We have worked very hard in keeping it a secret from you two. I thought for sure you knew what we were doing when you said you might have us do the kitchen for you. We had a great deal of fun with it, too."

"I can tell. It looks like you've spent a great deal of time in here getting it ready for us. This is the best surprise you could have given us. The room is going to be a big hit with my family, too." Beau wanted to invite them over tonight, but knew that without a fridge in the room, they couldn't keep anything cold. And without a stove, he'd have to microwave everything, and that wouldn't be good. "I'm going to have my family over as soon as the house is finished up. I'm betting that any day now we'll be thinking we're done and can relax."

"We are most rewarded by helping you two. You have made things very easy for us without overwhelming us." He thought about the sugar cubes that he'd purchased that were being delivered tomorrow for them all. Plus, with the new flowers that were coming up in the garden, they'd have plenty to eat and have treats as well. "Thank you for not being upset about the kitchen. It was fun for all of us to have a hand in working on getting it fixed up for you two. You're the best masters we've ever had."

He didn't particularly care for being called 'master,' but he'd talked to them about it before and hadn't come up with anything better for them. When he suggested they just call them by their first name, they said that was too familiar and wouldn't do it. He was going to have to think of something soon, or his brothers were going to have his head.

Chapter 4

Walking around the garden, Danielle couldn't believe how lovely it was looking. There was very little in the way of flowers this time of year, but she could see where the stones were in the garden and the planters, all lined up around the fountain, were looking good as well. She couldn't wait until spring, when the faeries promised her that things would start to come up and look beautiful. Then in the summer, things would be in full bloom all the way until fall, when the last of the flowers would be blooming.

"You like the garden? We still have plenty to do, but it is well on its way to being the showcase that it once was." She told Honey that she loved how they'd made it all new-looking. "It was easy once we got all the grass taken out and the bulbs given enough room to heal and become flowers again. In the spring, they'll push their stems out, and you won't believe how beautiful it will be with the butterflies and birds coming around to feast on the blooms. Some of us will be here to make sure that things are watered and working well together. I'm excited as well."

"I noticed that you've taken out the trees that

seemed to be growing at a fast rate here. Were they planted or just coming up on their own?" He told her that they were once weeds that had grown almost too strong to be in a garden. "You must let me know if you need anything removed that is larger than you can handle, Honey. I'd gladly pay for the removal rather than any of you be hurt."

"We were able to make it work this time, but I shall keep that in mind when we have to do the back garden. There are trees back there that have died and are now in the way of other flowers and bulbs." She told him to tell her which ones, and she'd have them taken out with a professional. "I believe that if you were to ask any of the Sheppards to help you, that would be all that it takes. They're strong men and will help you in any way that they can because you are their sister."

She didn't know about that, but she'd ask Beau about it. He'd know someone who could take them out if his brothers were too busy to help out. And from what she knew of them, they seemed to be busy all the time with one thing or another. She sort of envied them at their work. Danielle needed something to keep her from being at the house all the time. While she was glad that she was able to get the house in working order, it's all she'd been doing for a month. Even Beau would go and help his brothers when he was needed.

Filling out applications for the few jobs that were around town hadn't gotten her anything yet. But she also knew that she was new to this town, and they might not want to hire someone they didn't know. Being all right with that was fine, but she was no closer to getting a job than she had been before. Frankly, she was bored with housework.

Every day for a month now, she'd been working on the house. It looked like it was coming along, but there was still so much to do. When she thought about it, she realized that she had a lot more finished up than she'd thought. All of the third floor was finished and ready for furniture. The second floor only had the master suite to go. Now that there were bathrooms in every bedroom, too, she knew that cleaning them was going to be a chore. But having a single bathroom on each floor had to go. There were just too many bedrooms for a bathroom to handle them all.

The master needed to have the floors redone. She wanted to ask the faeries to do it; they did such a wonderful job in the living room, but they were working so hard that she didn't want to add to their workload. As it was now, she thought they were overworked and didn't know how to pay them. When Beau said he'd take care of it, she depended on him to do it. But so far, she'd not seen any kind of exchange of money for them to keep them going. A few blooms and sugar cubes didn't seem like nearly enough for what they were doing.

Going back into the house after her tour of

the gardens, she still couldn't believe how lovely the kitchen looked. With the appliances in place, Beau had been cooking them some fantastic meals. He was even leaving her something for lunch when he had to work with his family. That was the nicest thing he could have done for her because she was sick to death of sandwiches from the sub shop.

She'd finished the office just this morning. She'd not been joking when she told Beau that if it was paper, she would shred it. There was no point in leaving things to chance if she didn't have to. Knowing that someone could get all kinds of information from old mail, there was no way she was going to allow herself to be caught in that trap. It was something that she'd learned in college when she'd been there for business management classes. She missed those days of going to classes every day.

Danielle needed to get out of the house. And not think about working on it for at least twenty-four hours. Gathering up what she'd need to leave, she was at the door when she thought of something else. Calling for Honey, he came to her right away. It might have been her frantic tone, but he looked nervous when he flittered around the room in front of her.

"I'm going to go and find me something to do that has nothing to do with this house." He nodded. "While I'm gone, I want you to finish the house up. I know that I said I wanted to do it all by myself, but those days are over. Finish it up the way you think it needs to be done, and I'll be happy that I don't have to mess with it anymore."

"Yes, my lady. Does that mean the things that need to be repaired as well? There is still the matter of the leak in the basement that you said was too big for us to do." He looked like he thought that she'd been wrong on that as well. She told him everything. "Very good, my lady. You've made us very happy to serve you. It will be finished in no time at all."

Just as she was stepping out the door, she could hear the hum of wings. She didn't know what sort of mess she was going to be coming back to, but at this point, she didn't care. There were things that needed to be done, and she was sick of doing them. Thinking that she should have allowed them to do this at the very beginning, Danielle smiled when she thought of the look on Beau's face when he returned home to find things different than when he left.

The first thing she was going to do was get herself something to eat. She'd had breakfast hours ago, and now she wanted something for lunch. Someplace that had cloth napkins instead of paper ones that were in a holder. She also wanted a coffee. Something that she didn't need to read the directions on to make. Excitement ran over her skin as she made herself a mental note of what else she was going to get into today.

While waiting in line at the coffee truck that just happened to be in town, she thought of lunches that she'd been having with the other women of the leap. It had been fun, but she wanted to eat alone and enjoy herself by ordering what she wanted. She wouldn't admit this to just anyone, but she was intimidated by the other women because they seemed to have their lives so put together. She was barely holding onto her own sanity most of the time, and she was afraid to show them the real her when they went out. Today was for her.

"I have a question for you." She nearly screamed when someone spoke to her. "Are you all right? I didn't mean to startle you. It's Carrie. I'm Archie's wife."

"I was just getting out of the house for the day and was making plans to have lunch." She said she'd love to join her. "All right, but I'm going to be myself today. I'm sick of trying to handle the house and my emotions."

"I wouldn't have it any other way. I'll meet you at...where are we going?" She told her what she was doing right now. "Oh, I love their hot cocoa. I would love one if you don't mind. I'm nearly there anyway."

Danielle didn't know if she was disappointed or not about the company, but she wasn't going to change her mind now about her plans. Carrie would either like her or not. Today, she didn't care one bit. Tomorrow was a different story, but since she'd left the house this morning, she was going to have a good day no matter whose feelings she had to hurt to have one.

Carrie met her at the tables as she had gotten her the hot cocoa along with her coffee. After getting it and taking a sip, she wasn't sure that she liked it, but was going to drink the thing no matter what. She'd never been a big fan of coffee, and with all the things that were in this one, she was sure that she should have gotten one that was just plain instead of the one that she had.

"You said you were going to be yourself today. I wondered if you were playing along with us when we had lunch. Why are you holding back?" She told her. "I like you just fine, and I think that you're funny when you let go. From now on, be yourself. I know that I'd think you were fitting in rather than not."

"I don't fit in with you guys." She asked her why she'd think that. "I don't have anything in common with you guys. You're used to having money. I'm squeezing my money so tightly that it feels like it's not going to work for me anymore." She took another sip of the coffee and shoved it away. "That made more sense in my head than when I said it. I don't know how to spend money on things. This coffee is a prime example. I got it because it was expensive. I hate it. I should have stuck with something that I like rather than bother with the amount of money it cost me."

"Spending money is difficult for me as well."

She said that she didn't act like it. "Oh, but I do. When I go out to lunch with the women, I check the prices first before I order. I don't have to. Archie has assured me that we have plenty of money that we can be free with. I can't get over that."

"I've been making the faeries not help me with the projects around the house for fear of them wanting all my money. I don't know how that would work as they're just little people, but that's my fear. And since Beau is taking care that they get paid, now I worry that he'll be out of money too, and where will we be? How do they get paid anyway?" Carrie didn't laugh at her but told her that she did know the answer to that one. And she told her. "I can't believe that they like being paid by helping us. There has to be more to it than that."

"Sugar cubes and juice. I usually lay out some fresh fruit for them, and they love to nibble on flowers. But they feel helpful when you have them working for you, and that's all they live for is to serve." She laughed a little. "They also like to find things that they can barter with, like soda caps and cork. I had a lot of those left over from a project that I'd done, and they used them for a lot of things. Seats in their homes, I believe. And they love scraps of material of all kinds. They sew it into curtains and things again for their homes."

"I found some tiny safety pins in one of the drawers I was cleaning out, and one of them asked if they could have them. I had no idea what they'd use them for; they were still as big as they were, but I told them they could have them. I just remembered there were a lot of things like that. Things that they asked for, and I gave them to them. Is that all they want?"

"You have to make sure that they rest, too. Sometimes, if they have a large project to do, they'll do it until they're exhausted. I heard you have a lot of them at your home." She told her there were a couple of thousand still working in the house and that many more were in the gardens. "You more than likely have the happiest of all the pips that are in our homes. They love to work in gardens too. And they'll have your house in tip-top shape in no time."

"I told Honey when I left to finish the house. I hope that I didn't give him too much to do." She told her that since there are so many of them, they'd divide up the rooms between them and do them like that. "I just wanted it finished so that I can get on with my life. I think that Beau has been waiting for me to get sick of cleaning before he said anything to me about the faeries just getting it done. I can't believe I've spent this much time on the house and getting it ready when I could have been enjoying life instead."

"It sounds to me like you really need to get your life together, Danielle. And having the faeries do the house is the best idea that you've come up with." She said now she was having second thoughts. "I understand that. Let's go have some lunch somewhere so that you can forget you even have a house for a little while."

"I'd like that." As they made their way to the little diner that served the best burgers in town, she knew that she was going to feel guilty for a long time after giving the faeries such a large job to do. "I just hope they don't overdo it. They've been so kind to me so far."

~*~

Beau hated to go home tonight. He'd had such a long day that he just wanted to go home and relax for a little while. But until they got the house situated, there was no way that he was going to be able to sit on the new couch they had and put his feet up. The house needed to be finished soon, or he was going to suggest that the faeries do it all and upset Danielle.

He believed that she had the right idea about the faeries overdoing it with the house. But they were sad too that she was holding them back from getting it finished to please her. And they wanted her to be happy in the worst sort of way. Honey had spoken to him just this morning about the house being unfinished.

"She doesn't want to overwhelm you." He said that they were very underwhelmed right now. "I understand, but she has it in her head that the lot of you will hate her if she just tells you to finish the rooms. Danielle doesn't want any of you hurt or overworked by doing everything that you can to the house."

"She doesn't understand about the magic either. Not even her own." He'd noticed that as well over the past week. She was using her magic to bring her things, and she'd not noticed it as yet. He pointed it out to her, and she said that she just hadn't looked for whatever it was very well and found it. "She believes that we're just too small to handle any of the big jobs. That's why she is still thinking that the furnace will need to be replaced by someone her size. Also, did you know that she checks on us daily? To make sure that we're taking a break. It's difficult to do anything with her forever making us stop to rest every little bit."

Beau had laughed, but Honey hadn't thought it was funny. "I'm sorry. You do know that she means well, don't you? She just loves having you all around her. You might want to know that she thinks that you're not being paid. And that she believes that you will wish human money to work for her. I believe that is the biggest reason for the house not being done the way you can make it finished up."

"She has given us so much in the form of payment now. Did I tell you that she gave us some clips from the office? And some safety pens that we're using for all kinds of things. I believe, too, that she is saving things for us in the little jar she has on her desk. I found a stone in the collection that I'm using for my wall in my house. There are many things that she is leaving us to find, too." Beau thought that she didn't understand that was what she was doing, as it was just a habit for her to keep small things from the sweeper and being sucked up into it. "While in the kitchen, she gave us all the plastic wrapping that was around the fridge to take home. There was so much of it that we all got some of it if we wanted it. Do you believe that she thinks that's not payment enough?"

"I do believe that. She thinks of it as trash and not something that you might find useful. I'll have to explain that to her. What kinds of things did you use the stuff she leaves you around for? I'll tell her that when I speak to her tonight." He gave him a list of things that she'd left out for them and what they'd used them for. "This will be very helpful. Anything else?"

"The plastic had been a huge help in putting windows around our little dwellings. Also, it had made a protection from rain too for our roofs when it rained last evening. Why, just the other day, I used some of it to make a shiny ball for my children to play with. It's most useful to us. And the foam that was placed on the handles, I don't know what it's called, was perfect for making mattresses for our beds too." Honey was excited about the things that she'd given them. "I wish you would tell her how much she's paid us already. And the blooms that you put out and the sugar cubes have gone a long way in keeping our energy up and us working. I love the pits of chocolate you have given us as well."

"It's my pleasure." He had smiled at the little man and was glad that he'd come to him about the issue. Now here he was going home and would have to break the news to her that she was holding back the faeries from working by keeping them away from their need to be helpful.

Honey met him at the door before he was even inside the house. He thought for sure that something had gone wrong and that he was warning him about it. Or that Danielle had been hurt and was now bleeding all over the floor. He wondered if there was a fire raging on and that—

"There is nothing wrong." He let out a breath that he'd been unknowingly holding. "You look so upset that I wonder now if you've any idea what has happened today."

"I was going to talk to her tonight." He said that he'd thought that he'd already spoken to her. "No. She was still in the shower when I left today. I didn't get a chance to talk to her. What's happened?"

"The house is finished. Well, we still have to have knowledge about the rooms and how you want them set up. We even took care of the living room again, this time filling it all out with comfortable things for you to rest on." He asked what had happened that they had done this. "She told me to have the faeries finish the yard and the house, that she wouldn't be back for a while. I think she was getting as frustrated with the house as we were. And you."

"I didn't want her to hurt her feelings about getting it done." Honey told him that it was much too late now for her to change her mind; the house was finished completely. "Is she in the house now?"

"No sir, she went out this morning and hasn't returned as yet. She seemed sort of ready to get out of the house today. We'd been in the garden, I was giving her the tour of what we had finished, and she went into the house. A few minutes later, she told me that she was going out to finish the house while she was gone." He asked if she'd said anything else. "Only that she was sick of the house and wanted it done now. I asked her about the repairs, and she said that we could do it all to get the house in shape."

"Good for her. She must have gotten something in her ear that made her want to finish it. I'm so happy for her." He said that he was as well and was happy to have been able to do it for her. "I bet you are. I'm betting that you all wish that it was finished sooner so that you could go home."

"Sir?" He said that they'd been working so hard on the house for them that they probably wanted to go home to their families. "This is our home now. We have all become a part of the family that is the Sheppards' home. You wish to send us away?"

His voice trembled with hurt. Beau hurt too

from the sound of it. Trying to think of a better way to tell him that he thought they'd had homes, he was at a loss when the little man decided to go away, deeper into the house. Calling him back only served to show that he could see his tears now, and they didn't make him feel any better.

"I'm sorry. I didn't know." He told him it was all right. "No, it's not. I hurt you, and I'm sorry for that. I didn't know that you'd all be staying here. I was sure you had families to go home to and things that needed your attention elsewhere in the world. Doesn't Lily, the lady of the earth, need you for the flowers or something?"

"We were sent here to help the young miss and to stay to help her with all her needs. Lady Sunny said that we were to make her happy as we had made her when we helped with her home. It's a lovely home too." He agreed with him. "But she's been so sad of late. We were fearful of her not wanting us to help her. Then you wished to send us away now that the house is—there is so much to do when the children come along. As the house will stay in good repair, it will need updates to it in the future. New furniture and the like."

"I don't want any of you to leave. I know that you have families, correct?" He said that he had a very understanding wife who knew he was doing a wonderful job with him. "Bring them here. We'll find someplace to put everyone. Right now, I don't know where, but we will. Have your family and that of the other faeries bring their loved ones here so that you can be as happy as we can make you, too."

"If you're sure, my lord." He said that he'd never been so sure of anything in his life. "Very good. I will tell the others. Tonight, when the young miss comes home, you'll have to show her around the new home. We have made it the best that we can and repaired things that needed it too."

"Like, what did you repair? So that I can tell Danielle." He rattled off about a half a dozen things, like the leak in the basement wall as well as the air conditioner unit for the house. "Good. I think that this is perfect. Yes, Danielle will be so happy. Now I need to have a look at the living room and how it's finished. Then I'm going to wait for her to return so that we can look over the house together. You'll go with us, right? Point out the things that you did to the house to make it perfect?"

"It would be my pleasure, sir." After going into the living room, one of the faeries brought him a glass of water with ice. It was just what he needed then, and he was happy to have it. As scones were brought to him, too, Beau enjoyed a nice snack while waiting for Danielle to return. He only hoped she was in a good mood when he told her that he'd doubled, if not tripled, the number of faeries that were in the house now by inviting them all to stay.

Lying back on the sofa, he reached out to her. He would know if she was busy or not, but when she answered him with a wonderful 'hello', he thought her in a very good mood. He asked her what she was doing.

"Shopping for a baby gift for Sunny. She more than likely has a great many things right now, so I'm looking for something that she might not have. What are you doing?" He told her. *"Oh, a nap does sound good. I'm assuming that you're home by now? Right?"*

"I am. The faeries have finished the house, but I'm going to wait on you getting home before I have a look around." She told him that it was sweet of him, but he didn't have to do that. *"I want to. You wanted it finished, and it is, I've been told."*

"I was frustrated with myself. I should have finished it weeks ago. When you first moved in with me. So that we could spend some time getting to know each other. Instead, I was obsessing over the house that never seemed to be finished and missing life." He told her that it was all right that she needed to do what she wanted. *"I could have listened to you and not been as frustrated as I have been for the past week. Not anything to do with you, but just the house. It overwhelmed me a great deal."*

"I thought you were handling it very well. I never noticed." She told him that she was only frustrated after he left for work. *"Oh. I guess you would put on another*

face when I came home, too."

"Pretty much." They both laughed. *"I'm coming home now. I've had enough of a day off. I think I needed this more than I thought that I did. Maybe if I had taken some time off more than I had, I'd not have been so stressed out all the time. But knowing that the house is finished has taken a great deal of it off my shoulders. I learned a few things from Carrie, too, about the faeries. I've picked up a few treats that they can have tonight."*

"They like just about anything." She said that she went to the craft store and got them some quilt blocks so that they can use them. And some other tiny things she thought they might like. *"They'll love that. The pens that you gave them and the plastic from the stove have been a huge hit. They used them to cover their houses in the event of rain and other things, too."*

"I'm glad. Carrie assured me that they like things rather than payment too. And I didn't realize that they loved chocolate." He said that he only gives it to them as a special treat. *"Then they deserve it every day for the special way they've been treating me."*

"Come home, love. We'll go through our home together and be happy about it. I think we should order in too. To celebrate. How about that?" She said that was perfect. *"Good. I'll see you soon. And Danielle, I love you with all that I am."*

"I love you, too, Beau. I didn't know it until you just told me. But I do love you with all my heart. I'll see you

soon." He couldn't wait for her to get home and was excited to go through the house. But most importantly, she loved him, and he loved her. Nothing could stop them now. Not ever.

Chapter 5

Marsha was avoiding talking to her children because she was afraid that they'd tell her again that they didn't believe who she was. Rogen had been the worst at trying to convince, and now she was pissed off at all of them. She thought that they'd be thrilled to know that their mom was alive and around. But no, they were the most untrusting people that she'd ever met.

She wasn't really their mother, she thought with a smile. But she'd been working so hard at getting into their lives that she no longer believed anything but that she was — or at least she was trying to believe it all the time. She needed to get into their lives now more than ever. And their father was going to stay out of it, too.

Donald Watson had moved away when his wife had been killed. He didn't seem to be all that upset with her death either. It had occurred to her that they could have been having troubles at home, but the kids never mentioned it when she spoke to them at the funeral. In fact, they said very little when she'd been questioning them about her death. But now there was money to be had, and she wanted to be there to get some of it. Stupid people. Why didn't they believe her when she told them that she was their mother?

She'd gone to great strides in trying to look like her. The haircut alone had been costly to her, with the dye job included. Then there was the fact that she didn't wear any makeup. She'd made that mistake at the funeral in putting some on her face to make her look better. They wanted it off right then and there.

The day of her funeral had been a gloomy day, and the rain started just as they were leaving the funeral home and heading to the cemetery. She'd been assigned to drive the family limo and had thought they'd talk among themselves about what had happened. But no, they were as quiet as church mice. Not even offering up any conversation about anything in their lives.

Marsha had tried to get into a family once before. They'd been rich and had plenty of gossip to go around. But something happened when she was about to reveal herself, and she nearly lost her freedom. As it was now, she had to keep an eye out for things going on around her so that she'd not get caught this time. It was as easy as pie, she thought, to fool people into believing that she was some sort of relative from their past.

She'd done it before. Posed as one of the family members to a group of people grieving about their loved ones. It had netted her a great deal of money when she could prove beyond a shadow of a doubt that she was related to them. Not even DNA would stop her, as she had access to the body before it had been embalmed at the funeral home. When they'd ask for some proof that she was related, she would just pull out a sample of the dead person's blood and send it on its way. Every time, it would come back as a match to the family, and they'd pay her off to keep the nasty bit of a secret out of the papers. Posing as an illegitimate child always worked. But this time was different. She thought that she could pull off being someone they'd lost. And it would work too. She knew that she had all the information she needed from the funeral records.

That's where she'd gotten the phone numbers, off the paperwork. She'd gotten blood samples and DNA from the deceased. She knew their names and who they were married to from the paperwork that was to go into the paper. She only needed to look enough like her that they thought it was their mother after all this time. And that had cost her nearly all the funds she had left from her last scam. She might well have to do that again in order to keep up appearances with the Watson family and all their millions.

She was only going to do it as a lark. Have some fun messing with their minds. But then, recently, one of the women had married a Sheppard. And she knew them to have plenty of money to bring her into the family. The more research she did on her 'children', the more she realized that they had a bit of money too. But being married to a powerful and wealthy family was what sealed the deal for her, so to speak.

She didn't know which one had married Rogen, but she had a good idea that they were all as wealthy as the next. The houses that they'd had built were large as a mansion, and they seemed to have an endless supply of money when it came to helping the city in which they lived. Even Rogen had money to burn when she wanted it.

Marsha looked down at the picture she'd taken of the dead woman and then at the picture they'd been given to have her makeup and hair done right for the funeral, and knew she was a perfect match. Her hair had been the hardest to match with color. It was a dark hair that had these blue highlights throughout it. But because of the strange color it was, she'd needed to go to three different parlors to have it matched perfectly. But her hair had been the least of her problems. There was the tattoo that she had on her left shoulder that was difficult to match at all, and she still wasn't happy with it.

It had been a paw of some kind. Probably a dog or cat she'd been close to. The paw had been large and the colors difficult to match again, but how often when they ask to see a tattoo, she more than likely got when she was drunk and out on the town. Looking at it now, she thought that it was just too slanted to be on her shoulder, and it had healed incorrectly when she'd gotten it done. Some of the colors had faded and had blurred after it had healed, and it was what had her thinking it was a cheap tat that Marsha had gotten one night a long time ago.

She had all the confidence in the world that she could pull this off, and if she did, she was going to be set for life. She'd make good on her own promise to herself to get into the family, take as much as she could from them, and then 'kill' herself all over to do it to someone else's family. And if they brought up something that she didn't know about, it would be easy to say that it was from the accident that she'd been hit in the head when it had happened.

Tomorrow, she was going to see Calhoun Watson. He was the sappiest of the men in the family and would believe her if she told him that she was their long-lost queen or something. As it stood right now, she was going to keep her cool and just play right into his hands. Or he was going to be playing right into her hands. Either way, she was excited about this as she was the first time she'd scammed a couple that she was the husbands long long-lost daughter from an affair and needed to be paid off.

Actually thinking about it now, it had been twelve years now since she'd first started with her little games. The couple had divorced after she'd shown up and started her trouble for them. She didn't care one way or the other if they ended up separated or not. It was a very profitable game that she played with people that she saw while working at the funeral home.

She didn't work there anymore. After it came out that someone had been embalming people who were to be cremated, they went out of business. A shame that she had quite a thing going for herself. But charging people for those services when they specifically were told that it was direct cremation had gotten them into trouble with the board. Whoever that might have been.

Marsha had only been the hair and makeup artist. Or so they thought. But she did as much work as she could there to grab all the information she could about the dead. It was fun for her, really, another game that she played in not getting caught. And she never had in all the time she'd been doing this.

Picking up the phone, making sure she had the right number, she called the oldest son and told him that she wanted to meet with him. He didn't seem to be inclined, and she thought for a moment she was already being pushed out, but in the end, he said it would be all right. Good for him.

"I've been trying my best to get to you all, but I didn't know that you moved." That had been something that she'd not counted on when she called them. That it was going to take her some time to get to where they were living now. Not even the stupid farmers had stayed home to be called by her. "When I said I was in town, I didn't realize that you all no longer lived there. I was concerned about that."

"Concerned, why? So we moved? It's been over ten years since we were notified that you were dead." She didn't care for his tone and said that to him. "Well, since we're still trying to figure out how you survived being killed and embalming, I think we have the right to be snarly."

"You don't believe that I'm your mother?" He said no, that none of them did. "If I could just get to you soon, I'd be able to prove it. I'd ask you to ask me something that only I would know, but with the head injuries that I had during the accident, I'm afraid my memory isn't as good as it used to be."

"That's a good one. Are you going to stick with that story?" She decided that she wasn't going to try to get money from this one at all. He was just too mean to her. Telling him that she needed to go, he laughed harshly and told her to talk to him. "There is no telling what you can say to me to make me believe that you're my mother from ten years ago. I would ask why it took so long for you to get in touch with us. We've already figured out where you might have gotten our phone numbers. Unless that's the only thing you remembered."

"You're not very nice. I think I raised you better than that." Again, the harsh laughter that had her pulling the phone from her ear. "I'm going to hang up now and hope that you get better manners in the future. You shouldn't be talking to your mother this way."

"When I believe that you're my mother, I'll apologize. Until then, this is all you're going to get from the lot of us. None of us believes you're who you say you are. Not even dad." She asked when he spoke to their dad, fearful now that he might have given her away somehow. "He's here staying with my sister, that's Rogen in the event you're going to ask me what her name is. We've all been catching up and having a wonderful time. You're barely mentioned as a matter of fact."

"You're very cruel, aren't you?" He said again that when he believed she was his mom, then he'd apologize to her. "I believe you should be apologizing right now. I've never been spoken to that way in my life. And I am your mother."

"You'll have to prove it then. Right now, all I can tell you is that you'd better have all your information correct because we're not going to take this well if you're not her. Which I don't believe at all, so you know." She said that she'd gotten that from him. "Good. I don't want any misunderstanding when you come around and think that it's going to be all fun and games for you. Rogen is especially pissed off, and Sandy too."

"I've heard that Rogen recently married. And that Sandy's husband is on trial for murder. Seems like my little family could use a good person in their lives right now." He said it wouldn't be her. "We'll see about that now, won't we?"

"Yes, I suppose that we will." His laughter was getting on her nerves, but she was keeping her cool. If she lost her temper now, all her hard work would be for nothing. She needed to get where the money was, and they had a great deal of it. "I'm hanging up now. Don't call me again, whoever you are."

"And what will you say if I turn out to be your mother, like I've been telling you I am? What will you say to me then? An apology will not be enough from you." He asked her if she was talking about money. "Yes."

The phone went dead, and she was grateful for it. She'd lost her cool in that last question from him, and she needed to make him think that she wasn't there for just the money. She was, no doubt about that, but she needed to make them believe that she was their mother first and foremost so that she could get as much from them as she could.

She had to think about the conversation that she'd had with Calhoun. He was smarter than she'd given him credit for. She didn't know what he did for a living yet, but she had someone looking into that for her. It paid to have as much information as she could when infiltrating a family like she was doing this time. The rewards would be much better if she could get everything that she could about them. The next time she spoke to Calhoun, it would be in person, then he'd have to deny that she wasn't his mother to her face. Not that he was going to be able to. She was, after all, the real deal when it came to being his mom.

~*~

Rogen didn't like this. There was something very off about this woman that she couldn't put her finger on. Calhoun said that she was having trouble getting to them since they moved — he claimed that he thought she was begging for money until he pissed her off. That was something else he told her. Mother would have said something along the lines of his respect for her and that she was going to tell his dad. She seemed to be surprised that they'd even called their dad into this thing.

Then she said that he was going to have to give her money for the way that he'd treated her. Their mom wouldn't have demanded money; she would have told him that he was going to be beaten. She had never thought of them as too old to be beaten by their dad, and it mattered little that they were married, either. She would take care that they were punished for doing something against her.

There were just too many things that she said to Calhoun that didn't add up. Most of her problem had been that she didn't want to believe that she was their mother. And she wasn't. Dad had been present when the embalming had been done because she was a shifter. He would answer any questions that needed to be answered by being there.

There is no way that she could have survived that kind of work on her body, no matter what she was calling herself. The draining of her blood and then using the trocar on her would have killed even the strongest of shifters, much less a human being. What the embalmer thought he was embalming.

Dad had brought a lot of paperwork with him when he came to visit them. He had paperwork from the funeral home that stated that they'd received the body from the hospital on the night she'd been killed. Also, he'd been given a list of things that she'd had on her when she'd been in the accident that had killed her.

Then there was the fact that he'd been present at the embalming. That had taken a great deal of expense to have that happen, but Dad, even then, had been so grief-stricken that he wanted to make sure that she was dead when they buried her. The embalmer had even allowed Dad to take pictures of the marks that Mom had had on her body. The sigil that she had on her right shoulder was something that she'd gotten when she'd married their dad. A mark of the mates that they'd become, both of them were marked on their right shoulders. There was a police report, too, that had accompanied the body from the hospital that she'd been taken to.

"Do you suppose that she has the sigil on her

right shoulder?" Everyone turned to look at her, and she was slightly embarrassed. "I'm sorry. I just thought of that and wondered. If she is human—for whatever reason, I think that this is a human person trying to do this to us—would she have understood what the mark would mean and try to duplicate it?"

"That's a good point. I never thought of that. But why are you so sure it's a human?" She told them what she'd been thinking. "Again, I never thought about that. Her being able to lie to us is something that should have been the first thing that we thought of. We can't lie to one another."

No one said anything for long moments, and she was concerned they thought that she was wrong. They just had too much evidence to say that she was dead rather than being around them and causing trouble.

"I'm going to ask her about it if she calls me again. Or any of us should. That way, we can know for sure that she's lying. I have to admit, and only to you guys, that I hope this is Mom. I know it can't be, but I feel like I have plenty to say to her now that she's back in our lives. I have questions too." Rogen looked around the room, and it seemed that everyone was agreeing with her about their mom. "What do we do if she can't answer the question about the sigil? Do we just stop answering her? Or do we have her arrested as soon as she gets here? I have no doubt that she's on her way here as we speak. She wants something from us, and I have a feeling that it's money?"

"I do as well. She was practically begging me for money to get the rest of the way to us when I was talking to her." Rogen could see that Calhoun was still pissed off about the call that he'd gotten from her. "Even if she had come right out and asked for the money, I would have turned her down. I don't now nor will I believe that she's our parent. And that's something that I will take to the grave. As Rogen has said, she's human and we all just know it."

"I think we should have a list of questions that we ask her whenever she calls one of us. First and foremost, she should be asked about the sigil. And where it is. It should be easy for her to tell us, I'd think. Also, and this one is important too, why she waited. I no more believe that no one notified us of her being in a coma for the last ten years. Nor her waiting to get in touch with us. Sure, she could say that she didn't remember us because of the coma, but I just don't believe her." She looked around the room at the nodding heads of her family.

"Would compulsion work on her?" Calhoun and Rogen both said that it should, but you couldn't be sure if it worked unless you were face-to-face with her. "I'd like to have that arrangement made so that we can see for ourselves if she even looks like our mother."

"That would be easy to explain with the wounds from the accident, I think. She was banged up around the face when I saw her at the hospital. And since we had a closed casket, there isn't any way that we'd know if she was fixed or not." She thought about something else. "Mom's hair was unique, too. Remember how it had the blueish highlights of our kind throughout her hair. And the color was so beautiful, too."

"I think we should dig out pictures of your mother so that we can be ready when she gets here. I know that ten years can make a difference, but I don't believe that without a picture, we'd be able to see her for what she is. A fraud." Dad looked at her. "You have some of the pictures from the vacation that we took about a month or so before she died, don't you? Get some of those out and give them to the family. I might like to have a couple of my own. Even though it sounded like she didn't want me around, I'm still going to meet with this woman to find out what she wants. And if it is money, we'll have to turn her down like we know we should."

After everyone left, Rogen sat in the dining room and thought about her mother. If this woman was really their mother — and she didn't believe it for a second — then why now did she want to engage with them again? There was no reason for her to have come into their lives now when ten or fewer years ago would have been smarter. They were still grieving then, and it would have been easier for an imposter to have slipped into their lives. There were more questions than answers every time she thought of her and her reasons for coming back into their lives.

"Could it just be like she's saying? I mean, stranger things have happened, right?" She said that she supposed it could be true, but she didn't want to believe that her mother would be around after all that had been done to her. "Have you contacted anyone in your former home state? Maybe if she's there, someone can identify her for you."

"We have some neighbors looking out for her. I don't know what good it will do to have her coming around to them, however. Mom was never liked by a great many people." Weston asked her why. "She was mean and ruthless to people. I know that the Harts had a beef with her because she would forever park in their yard when she came home late from drinking. I always thought that she did it on purpose, but I never cared enough to ask. She was just mean to people who didn't stand up to her idea of human behavior. Which is to say she never liked humans at all. She thought that they were beneath her and all shifters, for that matter."

"Sounds like she was a great person to be around." They both laughed. "But seriously, have you given any thought to what you're going to do if she turns out to be just who she says she is?"

"No." Weston just nodded at her like he knew that's what she'd say. "There is just too much evidence to the contrary about her not being our mother. If she is, I'll be the first one to tell her how sorry I am that we disbelieved her. But I doubt that it will ever come to that. And we have a plan too. Whoever she calls next will ask her some questions about her body and the sigil that's on it."

"If she got the phone numbers where you think she got them, from the funeral home, then why hasn't she asked why she can't get in touch with Benson? I would think that would be the first thing that she asked." Rogen told Weston that she'd not asked and that to her was very telling. "Then there is Belinda. You said yourself that she didn't care for Benson marrying Belinda. You'd think that she'd mention something about that as well. To ask if they were divorced or something. Only a human would ask that question."

"You're right. I'm glad you thought of that." He kissed her on the nose. "What was that for? Are you hitting on me?"

"I am if that's all right with you. But now that we don't have to worry about the house any longer, how about we talk about having a baby? It's your body, so you tell me if I'm wrong in thinking that now would be a good time to start. We've got the sex part down pat, now we just have to wait until you're in heat again." She said that she wanted as many babies with him as they could have. "We're immortal, so that might be a lot more than you think." They both laughed.

"I would love children with you as soon as we can get pregnant. It'll give me something to look forward to before we have to deal with my mother's crap. I want them to be healthy and strong and know that they're loved by us. I know we have a lot to give them, but I don't want them to be spoiled either. Does that make sense?" He said that it did. Just because they could, didn't mean that they had to. "Good. On that we can agree. But having children with you might be the best thing that happens to this family. I know we'll have a lot of built-in sitters already."

"No kidding. They'll be fighting over watching the babies that any of us will have. And I think they'll all start having babies now that nearly all of us have mates." She agreed with him. "Now your mom shows up, and the shit will hit the fan with her." She asked him if he thought that it would. "I do. For whatever reason, I don't believe she's your mother either. I don't know why for sure, but things are just too...I was going to say weird, and that might be it. Why is she hiding herself in the shadows right now? Why hasn't she asked about Benson? I know that there were no grandkids when she died, yet but she could have asked about you guys. Has she ever once asked how you're faring? If you need anything from her? Those would be questions that I'd ask of my children if I hadn't seen them in a while."

"You know that's a good point. She has

never asked any of us if we're all right or if we need anything. I would have too had I believed that she was our mother. I would have been the first to send her money to get here, too, but she didn't act like a mother who missed her children." She kissed him on the nose for his help with those points. "Another thing is, and maybe you can figure this out, why didn't she want Dad around? I mean, you'd think that he'd be the one person that she could depend on to be there for her. I think you'd want to be there for me."

"I don't know, but I can guess." She asked him what he thought of. "He was the most intimate with her; he'd know all her personal traits and the way she said something. Did she curse? Would he have known that over you guys? The little details of her life would be something that he'd be able to pick up on. And I'm thinking that once she got you guys on board with her being who she said she is, then it would be easier to make him believe it."

"Mom didn't curse in front of his kids. Dad would know that too. Or if she only did it with him around." Weston nodded and told her that it would be things like that that would trip her up. "I agree. I should have had you at the meeting today with my family. You might have well hit right on it how we could tell. Does compulsion work on humans? And don't ask me why I think this is a human doing this. I just do, that's all."

"Compulsion works better on humans than it does shifters." She asked him why he knew that. "Because as a shifter, she would know that you could get her to tell the truth by using it, and she'd be prepared for it. You know, strengthen up her mind somehow to not give in to it."

"Whoever she calls next, and I'm doubting that it'll be me or Calhoun, the others are going to use it on her to get her to tell the truth. I think it would be better to do it in person, but that's just me, and we'd have to be face to face with her, and I'm not ready for that." She thought about it. "Though it would answer a lot of questions if she were to be here in person."

"Have you given any thought as to why she'd be doing this if she's not your mother?" Nodding, she told him what she thought. "That's what I thought too. Money. And since you've been 'married' to me for a few months now, it stands to reason she would have figured that out as well. More money would make a person, either a human or a shifter, do things that they normally wouldn't have done."

"She's done this before. That's another thing that I don't know why I believe that, but she's just too calm and assured in her talking to us for me to believe that she's not done this to someone else before. Some family that she's robbed of money by pretending to be a long-lost relative."

They talked about things for the rest of the

evening. Mostly, it was how their day had gone, and only sprinkling in a few bits and pieces about her supposed mother. Once they went to their room, she decided that it was high time they started having a baby in the family. She was ready when he was, and it seemed to be taking forever for her to ovulate. It wasn't as if they were wasting their time in having sex all the time. If she didn't get pregnant soon, it wasn't from lack of trying.

Chapter 6

Beau loved the advertising that Calhoun had done for them in terms of getting more people to come to the area with jobs. They'd had great responses to the little bit that they'd put out there before, but nothing like this. The advertising not only told that they were looking for new businesses to come to town, but also the perks that would come with them deciding to stay and build around here.

There were tax incentives that would make anyone want to put a new business in town. The construction companies that could work with them, should they wish to build. Even the state of the economy was there for them to see that they had plenty of people willing and able to work for them.

"I'm going to print you smaller flyers that you can send out in envelopes when you're addressing new people." Beau thanked him. "It's my pleasure. Business is booming right now for me. I never thought that I'd have so much work right away that I'd need to hire people to get it done. I've only been open three weeks so far."

"I know of a couple of graphic designers that

you could interview. They're good women, both of them are, but struggling to find a job in their area. One of them is married to a jag like us." He asked what he meant. "Nothing wrong. But she's married to a light colored jaguar like we are. I don't know why I thought that might be important to you."

"It is in knowing that she's a shifter. I like to hire from the leap, too. The people that I've met so far have been super nice and supportive." Beau told him that he'd thought that everyone was, but for a few of the elders. "They don't like change. I could have guessed that. When we belonged to the other leap, the elders were forever gripping around change. Like, it isn't going to be helpful for the leap to get modernized. I believe that it's the only way to keep up with the times, and we all need to do that at some point."

"I agree. We had classes set up for the elderly to learn how to order their groceries online. It didn't go over all that well. In fact, after the first class, it was shut down. They didn't want to learn how to do it because it was something too new for them. Some of them even stated that they have grandkids for that to go to the store for them." He asked how long they thought that was going to work. "Not long. For a time there, we had the highest age of people in a leap around. Now that Weston has taken over, we've gotten some newer shifters in the place, but he's still working on it. Sometimes it's an uphill battle."

"I would imagine." Calhoun smiled, and it looked sort of sly, like he knew something that he didn't. "I've been teaching my neighbor how to use the computer. I think I have her convinced that it's the only way to go if you want to keep up with things. She told me that she can't even make her remote work without one of her grandkids helping her."

"Maybe that's what we should have started out with instead of groceries. The remote control. More people might have enjoyed that." They both laughed, and he thought it was especially funny how all grown-ups needed help with their television controllers to make things work for them. "I'm going to bring that up to Weston and see what he has to say about it. He might well be on board with it rather than the other."

After Calhoun left him, still laughing about the classes, he looked over the advertisement again. It was bright and glossy, and he loved it. Now, if only they could get it in the hands of someone who really was looking for a place to build and bring jobs to the area, it would be worth it. As it was now, they were using them in the welcome center that saw a great deal of business when it was warmer weather.

The welcome center was a holdover from when the baskets were a big hit. They still were, but not on the scale that they once were when the founder had been alive. There used to be tour buses lined up along the street, as many as ten a day. Now they were lucky if they saw one once a week. It was sad, really, that it had run its course.

Their little town had benefited greatly from the tours. There were still shops along the main street in town, but they did more online business than with people coming to town to do the tours. He wondered what the town would look like if it were still going on like it had before. It would be great to see that, he thought. And instead of advertising for new jobs, he might be booking tours to have the basket people come into town to have a good time. Oh, what days those had been.

It took him most of the afternoon to get the new flyers that Calhoun dropped off folded. He was still working on getting all the equipment that he needed to run a successful business, so folding them was one of the things that he didn't mind doing. Besides, he loved the way they looked when they were stacked all folded up like they were. The first hundred he was going to drop off at Weston's office so that they could get them mailed out to go to prospective businesses.

He and Danielle were loving their new home. It had been finished up, thankfully, but the faeries and they were having a good time filling out the spaces that were there with little things that they'd picked up here and there. They'd been putting pictures in a pile on his new desk that they wanted to frame, and last night they started on them. He'd not realized what a few family pictures could do to a room once they were hung. It looked like someone cared enough to have family around them at all times.

He paused in going out the door of the office he'd been working on when he saw a stranger across the street. Beau had lived in this town for his entire life and felt assured that he knew everyone around, so when this woman looked like she was trying to find an address, he decided to wait until she asked him before he volunteered any information. He knew all about Rogen's non-mother.

Going out the door with his back toward her, he locked up before he heard someone behind him say 'Excuse me'. He was willing to ignore it for a while, but it wasn't in him to be rude. Turning with a smile, he asked what he could do for her.

"I'm looking for my children. I've not seen them in a while, and I was trying to surprise them with me showing up." He asked how old her children were, knowing full well it was adults she was talking about rather than children. "Oh, they're about your age. Maybe a little older. It's been a while since…well, they just moved to this area and I just arrived."

"I don't know any strangers in town if they just moved here." She looked frustrated with him, and he was all right with that. "What are their names, and perhaps I can find them for you. Or at least point you in the right direction as to where they might be."

"Watson is their last name. I have four boys and two daughters. My daughters are construction workers of all things." He nodded, not giving anything away. But he did reach out to Rogen and let her know what was going on. "Their names are Rogen and Sandy. The boys are Calhoun, Benson, Tommy, and Edward. Tommy and Edward are farmers. I don't remember what kind they are."

"What does she want?" He told Rogen that she was looking for her children. *"Do me a favor and tell her to fuck off. Not really. I'll do that on my own. Is there anything about her that you think I should know?"*

"She's human." Rogen didn't say anything while Marsha was going on about her kids and what she thought they did for a living. *"Also, you should know that she's unaware that Benson is dead. She named him as one of her children who should be around here."*

"I guess that sort of seals the deal on her being our mother. I was...never mind. I'll be there soon. If she gets away from you, no matter, I'll find her." He told her not to do anything stupid. *"I already did that when I sort of hoped she might be our mother."*

"Do you know my family?" Now that Rogen was coming, he thought that he should just tell her the truth. So he told her that he did know them all. "Oh, good. I was hoping to find them around here. I feel like I've been looking forever. Can you point me in the right direction?"

"Sure, but if you wait right here, Rogen is coming. She was supposed to meet me here." A small lie, but it was better than the truth right now. He saw the other woman coming toward him with all her family. It was going to be a showdown, it looked like. Even the mister was with them. He did wonder how she'd gotten them gathered up so quickly and realized they were probably at her home, still talking about her. Beau decided to stick around in the event they might need a cooler head. "It looks like your search is over."

Beau thought that she said something like 'oh fuck', but couldn't be sure since Rogen started speaking to her from a distance of about ten feet. The others formed a circle around their 'mother', and it didn't look all that good for Marsha or whatever her name was.

"You don't look a thing like our mother, just so you know. Your hair is all wrong." Rogen's hair was the same dark shade as a jaguar's in that it had the small blueish spots in it. "It's about as wrong as your face is."

"I don't know what you mean by my hair being the wrong color." She said she didn't say color, but that was it too. "It's been ten years, how can you be so sure? It looks the same as yours, but for a little lighter."

"Benson is dead. You might well have not known that since you're not our mother." She asked Belinda what had happened to him. "He was murdered along with my two children for money. Is that why you're here? Money? Well, you're not going to get anything from us."

"You're very hostile towards someone you've not seen in ten years." Calhoun said that it was the first truthful thing that she'd said all morning, as they had never met her before today. "I'm your mother. I even have the tat that is a paw print."

"Let's see it." She bared her left shoulder, and Rogen was shaking her head. "It's not a sigil but a real tattoo. Not to mention it's on the wrong shoulder. It should be on the right like it is for our dad."

"No, it's the left. I remember that." She told her that she remembered incorrectly. "I know what I know. And this isn't getting us anywhere. I've come all this far to see my children, and they're acting like I've committed some sort of crime. I think that we should regroup and meet up later. Perhaps in a better setting, like one of your homes. You all do have homes, don't you?"

"Yes, and you're not invited to any of them." Donald kept staring at her, and Beau wondered what he was thinking. When Sandy spoke again, it was as if they had all decided that whatever she said was going to be the way things went. "We can meet up later, but it won't be in our homes. I don't particularly want you in my home because of your cruelty. And there is no doubt to any of us that you're really her. You can't be."

"I'm your mother, and I can't believe that I raised you to be like this to me. I do have some memory loss due to the accident, but that doesn't explain why you're being cruel yourselves. I've never been talked to like this in my life." She looked at Donald, the only person who hadn't said a word to her. "What do you have to say for yourself? Or is the usual way that you do things just sit around and wait for someone to tell you what your opinion will be?"

"I know who you are." She said that finally someone believed her. "I didn't say that. I just know who you are. You're that woman from the funeral home. The hairdresser."

If he'd not been looking right at her, he might have missed her going pale. As it was, her cheeks brightened in anger, and she slapped Donald. As soon as Rogen went on the defensive to save her father, Beau stepped in front of her and stopped her.

"She's not worth whatever you have in your mind." Rogen glared at him and told him to move through clenched teeth. "Not until you realize that you'll go to prison and never see Weston again, other than through bars."

For a few minutes, he didn't think she was going to heed his warning. But when she took a step back, he did as well. There was no point in pissing her off more by crowding her. She was a jaguar same as him, and it would be bloody on his part if he had to tangle with her. But he'd never harm her, not if he could help it.

~*~

Marsha hadn't counted on a war between them. She thought that she might be better off leaving and regrouping for another scam. These people were insane if they thought that she'd stick around and talk to them again. How could she have made so many mistakes as she'd made in this one scam?

The tattoo was on the wrong shoulder? How could she have messed that up? Then she remembered that she'd taken a picture of it with her camera, and it had rotated the shoulders so that it looked like it was on the left. That little bit of information had come to her when she was trying to get away from them.

Then there was Donald. How did he know after all this time that she was the hairdresser at the funeral home? There was no way that he could have remembered her. And when he said that, why did he sniff the air like she smelled or something? That was only the tip of the shit that she'd done wrong. While Rogen was being talked down from trying to kill her, the others had shouted out other things that they noticed about her not being their mom.

"Like, how does me being human even factor into all this?" She asked herself that question several times since she left them standing there. "Aren't we all humans?"

Were they humans? There had been no

indication about them being shifters when she'd seen them at the funeral home. No one had mentioned to anyone in the car to the funeral or gravesite at all that they were anything but humans like her. If that was the reason that they knew she wasn't their mom, then she needed to get out of town quickly and hide. But if even a small fraction of what she'd heard about shifters was true, then they could find her no matter what. Especially since she'd touched Donald.

"Hitting him was a mistake." She could tell things now that she wasn't around them that she shouldn't have fucked with this family. They were a dangerous situation that she didn't need to be around.

It took her nearly two hours before she was calm enough to deal with her situation and get her ass moving out of town. She needed to get as far from the family as she could. How could something that she'd worked on for ten years go so horribly wrong? Well, she's learned her mistakes and now she was going to be better the next time she tried to scam people about their loved ones.

Would she stop? Hell no. It was a good money maker that she loved doing. No one was going to have her arrested if she failed, like she did with this family, but she was going to be a note in their lives and nothing more. It would be too embarrassing for her to be arrested, as she'd taken them for quite a ride so far.

"Well, not a ride for them." It had only taken

them about thirty seconds to realize that she wasn't going to get any payday from the Watsons. Even with the backing that they had from the Sheppards' family, she'd not want to be an embarrassment to them either. They'd just write it off as a lesson learned and be done with it. Laughing, she wondered if she could get some money out of them for being quiet on her end. "No, I'd better not press my luck with them anymore."

As she was packing her clothing, getting ready to leave as soon as she could, she thought about all the time she had wasted on this group. It was time and money well spent except for the tattoo. How had they been so sure that it wasn't on the left shoulder? Oh well, it was done now, and she was going to move on. She only hoped that they did too. There was no point in their being petty and having her arrested at this point. It would just be an embarrassment for all parties concerned. Just as she was closing up her luggage, a knock came at her door. She opened it with a bright smile that faded away when she saw the police there.

"What can I do for you, officers?" They said they were there because of fraudulent behavior on her part. "I'm sorry. It was just a misunderstanding on their part. I didn't do anything wrong."

"They said that you scammed them into thinking that you were their long-dead mother. That's about as fraudulent as you can get." She said that it was a misunderstanding. "Did you or did you not pretend to be their mother on several occasions. And did you or did you not tell Beau Sheppard that you were their mother looking for them?"

"Yes, I did that, but I was just playing a game. It's something that I do." She had hoped they'd understand, but they didn't seem to be getting it. "You see, I'm packing up to leave now. It didn't end the way that I hoped that it would, so I'm packing my bags and getting out of town. There was no reason for them to call you on this."

"I'm afraid that they didn't care for your little game. I'm going to have to take you in for questioning." She told him that there was no reason for that, and she was leaving right now. "I'll say when you can leave, and it won't be today. Come along nicely, miss, or I'll have to put you into cuffs."

"This isn't right, you know." She told them that she'd go with them, but they'd better have all their ducks in a row about detaining her unlawfully. "I'm not even sure why they're bothering with me. They saw through my deception, and I left them. It was all a game I was playing."

"What was your reward if you won?" She knew better than to answer that question, so she just went along with them to the car. Being put in the back seat, she thought of all the ways that she could countersue them and couldn't think of a single reason why they were doing this. There wasn't any harm done in her playing around with their emotions. These people needed to get a grip on their lives if they thought that having her arrested was the way to go. "You'll be put into a cell until such time that the Watsons and the Sheppards can come in and write out a report in pressing charges against you."

"I think there has been a mistake about all this. They have to be told it was just a game, and no one gets arrested for playing a game. My goodness, if they lose at cards, do they have the other party arrested, too?" He said this was different and that she'd messed with their lives. "In a game. When are you going to get that through your thick head that I was only messing with them? And since they figured it out, there was no harm, no foul. That's the way a game works when you — I'm not pressing any charges against them about me losing all my money in setting this all up, am I? No, I'm not. What a bunch of sore winners."

She was put into a cell and told that someone would come and talk to her soon. Also, the judge wouldn't be in until Thursday. It was Friday today, so she'd have to wait an entire week to have some judge throw this out of court because it wasn't anything to be upset about.

Her only recourse was to talk to the Watsons. There had to be a way for her to talk to them and tell them how it had only been a game that she was playing, and that she played like this all the time, and no one got upset for her winning. Of course, she'd have to give them names, she thought, and that wouldn't go over too well if they checked into things. The families that she'd scammed before would be told about her game, and they might be as upset as the Watsons were.

"This was all just preposterous. I don't know what to tell them that will make them back off, other than what I've been saying all along. It was just a game that I played on them. And they won." Sitting on the cot in her cell, she looked around. "This place needs an update. No way are they allowed to keep prisoners in a room like this one and get away with it. There is no way."

It was nearly dark in the room when someone came to see her. They had a tray with them, so she assumed that they were going to feed her. Since no one had asked her what she wanted, she was going to turn it away in favor of something else to eat. In a cell like this, there was no way that the food was going to be edible anyway.

"I was going to give myself a treat tonight and have a large pizza." She, the woman cop told her that she was only getting what was being served. "You can take it back and bring me something else then. I'm not eating whatever is on that tray. It can't be as good as the pizza I was going to get, and that's final."

The tray was set on the floor and slid under the bars. She didn't even bother looking at it and slid it back. Without a word from her, she turned on her heel and left the meal there as well as the scent of it behind. She'd teach them a lesson about herself. She'd not eat at all and see where that got them.

By the time another officer came and got the tray picked up, it was getting really dark in the hallways. No one had come to talk to her, and when she asked the officer when that was going to happen, he just ignored her and kept walking. People were rude around here, and she didn't much care for it.

She was brought a uniform, she was told, and she had to put it on. It was a putrid green color that made her sick when they tossed it at her. When she asked when someone was going to talk to her, she was told that she could make one phone call, and she'd get it when someone could come and fetch her.

"Fetch me? I'm not an animal like the Watsons are." She wondered if the Sheppards were as well and thought that it had some merit to it. "Where are the all-mighty Sheppards? They're pressing charges against me, too, right? I want to have my call now."

Who would she call? She didn't have a clue. She didn't have an attorney on speed dial. The only time that she'd ever used one was when she had had one of the college students at the university read over the contract she'd had for one of her scams. She supposed that she should stop calling them scams and continue to call them what she had in the past, and call them games. That's all they were to her. A way to play with people's lives, make a few bucks, and move on to the next game.

Messing with people's lives was easy, she thought. Of course, she only had two more DNA tests to use, and she thought that they might well be too old for her to use nowadays. She didn't mean that the DNA might be too old, but the people that she was going to scam might be too old and perhaps dead by now. She should have thought of that before and wondered why she'd not.

"Damn it. I need to keep better notes." She did wonder if she could get into the business of funeral hair dressing again. It had been an easy few bucks that she'd make on hair and makeup. She'd have to do something if she were going to be playing games in the future.

At just after ten, she was taken to a payphone to make her call. Asking for and receiving a phone book had been her next question, and she had to look up someone to come and help her out of this mess. Not that she thought it was going to be that big of a deal, once the judge heard her side of the story, he'd dismiss everything and allow her to go on her way. But she could only find two attorneys in the phone book, and both of them were taking on new clients. She called the first one to see if he could help her.

After telling him about the game she'd been

playing, he told her that he couldn't represent her. He said that she'd been too cruel about her 'game', which he made sound like she'd killed someone, and should be behind bars. The second man she called told her that he'd not represent her either and simply hung up on her. Didn't these people understand this was just a stupid game and that the other party had won? Christ, it was like the whole world had gotten a rod up their asses and didn't understand something that was funny anymore.

"Now what do I do?" The officer with her told her that she had to go back to her cell. "Just how long am I going to be there before someone gets their head out of their asses and realizes that this was just a fun game that I was playing. I'm the one who's out a lot of money and time, not them. What did they have to spend with me, twenty minutes? Less than that? And if you think about it, they should be arrested for not telling people that they weren't human. That should be the law about them."

"There is no law about people being human or not." She told her that there should be, and she'd not be in jail like she was. "Had you not messed with people's emotions, then you'd not be in jail. Don't forget that you lied to them about being their long-dead mother."

"That's the fun part for me. No one understands the game that I'm playing with people. It's all fun and games." She said, until someone gets hurt. "They weren't hurt by this. They never believed that I was their mother from the first time I spoke to Rogen. She's sort of a bitch if you were to ask me."

"No one asked you anything." The officer told her again that she needed to put on the jumpsuit that was given to her. When asked what they'd do to her if she didn't, she was told that they'd undress her and then put it on her. The hard way. "And it will matter little if you're hurt or not when we dress you either. I'd suggest that you put it on so that no one has to dress you. It won't be easy on you."

"We'll just see about that, won't we?" The smile that she was given didn't feel right, and she stood there with her chin up, daring her to call someone into the cell to get her dressed. As soon as the door to the outer offices was closed, she was plunged into darkness so dark that she couldn't see her hand in front of her face. "I hate this place."

Chapter 7

Danielle was sick of sleeping alone. She wanted someone to snuggle up with and be warmed by them. Beau was being a gentleman, and she was sort of sick of that, too. He'd been so polite with her that she wanted to bash his head in and make him see reason. Whatever that reason was, she didn't know, but she was getting frustrated with him and his politeness. She just needed a way to make sure he understood that she was ready for him to come and have lots of sex with her. But how to make that happen?

She supposed that she could just come right out and say she wanted him. But that didn't seem like something that she'd do. She'd always been sort of shy about sex and the way it worked. Like it was a job or something. There was a time in her life when she was sheltered away from sex, and that had been her undoing when it came to dating. She just didn't know how to be sexy when it came to having someone find her alluring.

Being more of a tomboy, she'd never grown up where things made her feel like one of the girls. She had always wanted to hang out with all of the boys around town. She played football in the fall with them, baseball in the spring, and sometimes she'd go to the movies with several of them just so she could see a movie when they did.

While later she did understand the difference between boys and girls, and had even started dating when she was a teenager. But her formative years had been ruined by hanging out with the boys who had played with her older and younger brothers when they'd been out and about around town. Not only did she not know how to be sexy, but she didn't know how to make sure that someone knew that she wanted sex, too.

Beau came into the kitchen with her and started drying the dishes as she washed up. He'd cooked, and she had promised to do the dishes. She didn't realize that he meant to help her out with them, too, and was glad for it. She asked him if she could ask him a question.

"Sure. Anytime. I have a couple of questions for you as well." She told him to go first. "All right. Today, when I was in town, I saw you at the bank. Did you sign all the paperwork that was there for you to sign? That puts you on the deed to everything that I have, and I wanted to make sure you got the credit cards."

"Yes, I got everything signed the way I was supposed to. They told me to sign the paperwork with your last name. So I signed it, Danielle Sheppard.

Right?" He said that was great. "And I got the credit cards. I had no idea there were so many that I'd need."

"For the most part, only a couple are needed, but we get good discounts for using the store cards in the store when we're there. No biggie if you don't use them, but it's nice to have them around when you need them." She told him that she'd just use the store ones in town when she went, and the others when she was ordering online. "Good idea. It's best to have a credit card with insurance on it in case something goes wrong."

"What else did you want to know?" He had to think before asking her, and when he did, she had to laugh. "Yes, I loved dinner. It was better than I thought it would be when you told me we'd be having fried eggplant. I'm not very good at trying new foods. But I loved it. I'd eat it again whenever you cook it."

"Good to know. Sometimes people will have fried eggplant instead of meat. I don't know if I'd go that far or not, but it's really good." He put the last of the dishes in the cabinet. "Now what did you want to ask me?"

He was drying the glasses that they'd used when she blurted out that she wanted to have sex with him. She also mentioned that she was sick of waiting, but didn't look him in the face when she said that last part. When he lifted her chin up and had her look at him, it was all she could do not to run from the room and hide.

"I'm not going to be any good at sex. I like it all right, but I'm sort of selfish, I've been told. Actually, what I've been told is that I'm too needy and selfish about my needs over anyone else's. I suppose that's right, but he was just taking too long to get to the end, so I'd just take over and do it myself. Why are you laughing?" Beau was laughing hard while she stood there waiting for him to stop. "I don't think this is the least bit funny. I'm trying to tell you why I want sex, so if you're going to laugh at me, I'm going to find someone else to make love to me, and that will be all on you."

"No. Please don't look for anyone else. I'm sort of a jealous lover, and I'd hate to have to kill someone over you. I would, but I'd rather not be in prison for having to kill someone who wasn't fast enough for you." She knew that he was making fun of her, but she couldn't figure out what it was that he was doing. "I promise you I won't make you wait until the end. But if you ever want to take over, you go right ahead, and I'll be happy."

"You're making fun of me, aren't you?" He promised her that he wasn't. "I don't know why, but I don't believe you. Why are you teasing me right now?"

"Because I find you to be a delight." She didn't know what that meant either, but decided that she wouldn't have sex with him ever. He was making fun of her, and she didn't think that was right. "You're beautiful when you're flustered. I think that I could get used to this, while we talk about sex."

"I don't want to talk to you anymore." He teased her enough that she smiled at him. "You're not very charming. I hope no one told you that you were. You're sort of mean if you want to know the truth of it."

"I'm sorry. Very sorry, as a matter of fact." He put his hands on her hips and turned her toward him. "I'd love to have sex with you. However, I think I prefer the term making love with you." She asked him what the difference was. "One is just two people getting their rocks off, the other is a night of bringing each other to peak several times over simply because you love the way they look when they're coming. I'd like to bring you to peak several times while I watch you. I'd also like to taste your flesh. And anything else that I can sink my teeth into on your body."

He moved his mouth along her chin to her throat. Once there, he began nibbling on her skin like she was a meal that he really was feasting upon. Her skin heated up, and she was glad that she was standing; she might well have fainted right out of a chair had she been sitting.

When he turned her around so that her ass was right at the counter, she let out a little yelp when he lifted her up and put her onto it. Not sure what to do with her hands, she put them on his shoulders and looked at him. She could see his gorgeous eyes this close up and couldn't believe the shade of blue that they were. Simply beautiful.

This time, he put his hands on her waist and, using his thumbs, he rubbed the bottom of her breasts. She could feel her nipples getting painfully hard while he did that, and she wondered what he was going to do next to her. It wasn't until he cupped her breasts that she knew he was going to take her right there on the countertop in the kitchen. And she was going to love every second of it.

Putting her hands on the counter behind her, she watched him unbutton her blouse. The way he was taking his time made her think that he'd done this before. But she didn't want to think of him being with other women, so she watched as he slowly moved the tiny button from her blouse through the little hole that held it in place. She would never remove her blouse again without thinking of him doing it to her today.

Once her blouse was open, he didn't pull it apart like she thought he would, but moved his fingers along the top of her bra over her breasts. When the blouse came open, he leaned in and licked the area where his fingers had been, then blew a warm breath over the trail. Christ, it nearly made her come with just that movement.

Taking her blouse off her shoulders, he pulled

it down to her hands that were still on the counter. Taking his time, he unsnapped her bra from the front and again left it the way it was. When he put his fingers in her pants, just at the snap, she let out a long breath that she'd been holding and closed her eyes. She was nearly ready to help him remove her pants when he gently ordered her to stay the way that she was. While he was taking his time with her, she couldn't help but want him to go slower so that when she did come, and she would, she'd have a climax that beat all others that she had.

She was out of her pants in minutes and enjoyed the freedom of the room with him there with her. She'd never been naked outside the bedroom or bathroom, so this was a new thrill for her. Even as she sat there in her panties and open bra, she would catch her breath every time he touched her skin. His fingers were so warm, and her skin felt chilled.

As he leaned in to kiss her, she felt his cock at her pussy. Even through his pants, she knew that he was thick and hard. The kiss was gentle and warm, his tongue traced the inside of her mouth, each dark place that she knew tasted of him. She wanted more of him, but was forbidden to touch him just yet. This was so exciting to her that she thought for sure that she was soaking the countertop with her warm juices. When he pulled her forward on the counter, she wrapped her legs around his hips and moaned when he rocked into her.

With her legs wrapped around him, he stepped back and reached for his belt. She hadn't noticed that he wore belts all the time, but thought that it was a way to torture her more when all she wanted was him. As soon as he had his pants undone and pulled to his thighs, Danielle reached for his cock and wrapped her hand around him.

"Christ," He hissed as she touched him. When he took another step back, she pulled him forward and guided him to her sheath. "I won't last long if I enter you now."

"Please." He moved forward, and she could feel his cock at her entrance. With her hand still wrapped around him, she moved herself to a better position as he took another step toward her. As soon as she could feel his heat where she wanted him, Danielle let him go and moved her hips in a way that took him inside of her. "Oh, Beau, yes."

Neither of them moved as they were attached at the groin. She could feel herself adjusting to his size and loved the feeling of him filling her up. As soon as he moved, just an adjustment to his hips, she came so hard that she nearly bucked him off her. It was more than she could have hoped for. Then he started moving in and out of her.

Cupping her ass, he pulled her off the counter and took her to the wall behind him. The three or so strides were enough to make her see stars. It felt so good. As soon as she was pressed against the wall, he started fucking her like he was never going to quit. Every part of her body felt like he was fucking it, and she held onto his shoulders or she would fall to the floor.

His hands on her ass were tightly massaging her. She knew she was going to be bruised tomorrow, but she found that she didn't care. Right now, they were both having the time of their lives, and she didn't care if tomorrow never came for them. As soon as he stiffened inside of her, she closed her eyes tightly. Whatever was coming, she was going to be prepared for it. When Beau threw back his head and cried out, she leaned into his throat and bit down hard enough that she was rewarded with a mouthful of his hot, spicy blood. It brought her so hard that she had to hang on or pass out from the sensation of coming apart and being slammed back together in seconds. Christ, she couldn't hang on to her consciousness any longer.

~*~

Beau was quite proud of himself as he watched over Danielle while she rested. She'd fainted, and he was never so proud of himself as he was in that moment. But still, he watched over her just in case something else happened to her while he waited. Taking her warm hand into his own, he kissed the back of it and put it back under the light blanket that he'd tossed over her when he'd put her into bed.

Getting up when he started to feel like he needed to join her in bed, he went to the window and looked out over the expanse of their backyard, and noticed the big barn as well as someone out mowing the lawn. He watched them doing the yard for a few minutes when he heard a slight sound from behind him. Turning, he was able to watch Danielle sitting up and lying quickly back down on the bed.

"Are you all right?" She glared at him, which made him laugh. "I know how you feel. You got a bit more magic. Since I'm used to having it, it didn't hit me as hard as it did you."

"How about if you come over here and let me hit you as hard as this has me?" She laughed but held her head. "I feel as if I've been run over in a good way. If that makes any sense."

"It does actually. But really, how are you feeling?" She said she was fine so long as she didn't move very much or very quickly. "Good. I guess that's some improvement. At least you're sitting up now. When you passed out on me, I was terrified at first."

"At first? Then what happened?" He told her that he'd been proud of himself. "Proud of yourself for rendering me unconscious? That sort of sounds a little sick if you... Wait, I guess I can understand what you mean. You did make me out of it for a while. Good job."

"Thanks. But next time I'd like to be in a bed. I'm a little sore on the backs of my legs and shoulders." She asked him if she'd hurt him. "I'm not going to answer that on account of me being so proud of the fact that you were out for a bit. That sort of defeats the purpose of being proud of myself."

"You're strange. Did you know that?" He grinned at her and agreed with her. "Good. I don't want anyone to let you think that you're anything but strange. Very strange."

"If you're feeling up to it, I'm starving. Would you like to go out and get some dinner?" She said that sounded good and started to get out of bed. She was still a little lightheaded, but she got to the bathroom with his help. When she claimed she wanted a shower, he said that he'd join her as he was feeling the need for one as well. They took a quick shower together, and he got his back scrubbed when he did the same for her. "You're so lovely, Danielle. Did anyone ever call you a shortened version of your name?"

"No. My grandda did for a little while, but he died when I was four. He called me Dani. But it didn't catch on, and I've been Danielle my whole life." She dressed in a pair of jeans and a sweatshirt to go out with him when he told her that it was going to be casual. "What about you? Did anyone ever call you Bo?"

"No. I've been Beau just like you have been Danielle, your whole life." She thought that it was a good name and asked him where he'd gotten it. "My mother didn't care for shortened versions of names. The only reason that Archie was called Archie is because my dad's name was Archibald. She thought that Beau was short enough as it was, and no one would try to shorten it. However, for a whole year in grade school, this kid kept calling me Bo-Bo. Thankfully, it never caught on."

They talked about his brothers all the way to the little diner that was on Forty. It was good hot food, if not a little greasy. But it stuck to your ribs so you'd not have to get something else to eat in a couple of hours to appeal to your stomach because you were hungry again.

Both of them got burgers and shakes to eat. Then, for dessert, they were able to get themselves the last of the pie from the day. It was lemon ice box pie and cherry that was left, and they both enjoyed it to the max. Beau thought that the cherry should have had ice cream on it, but they were out, so he had to settle for just plain.

After they were finished, they walked back home and got into the house just as it started to rain. He hated rainy days in the fall. It made everything a mess. Nor did he like the wet leaves on the street; they made the road slippery, and he was always fearful of an accident happening when the roads were like that.

"It looks like it's set to rain all night." He agreed

with Danielle as they cleaned up the mess they'd made in the kitchen. As they were wiping down the counters, all he could think about was how much he'd enjoyed their lovemaking and was glad that they were finally going to be sleeping together.

He had to refrain from trying to get Danielle to go to bed at eight. He just wanted to sleep with her tonight and wake up with her by his side in the morning. When they finally did go to bed at ten-thirty, he was so exhausted that he nearly forgot they were going to sleep in the master bedroom as their first night together. Getting into the big bed made him appreciate the smaller bed he'd been sleeping in until now. Beau was lucky that he'd fit in the smaller bed he realized now that he had a bigger bed to compare it to.

"Do you have to work in the morning?" He had to think for a moment and told her that he did until noon. "I have to meet with your sister, Sunny. She's going to show me how to use some of the magic that I got when we first started seeing one another. I guess now there will be more, right?"

"Yes. For both of us. The one thing that I might enjoy as much as you do is not having to change when we get out of the shower. We can think of something to wear, and we'll be wearing it. Archie said that it was his favorite bit of magic. I can see myself using it for all kinds of things. Like having to change to go out to dinner. Or just getting out of the shower in the morning. What about you? Do you think you're going to use it all that much?"

"I don't have to shift or anything, but like you, I can see myself using it if I have to change for a meeting that I forgot about. Also, if I get something on me. That would be very handy." He teased her about getting something on her and said he'd gladly lick her clean. "Behave. I'm still sore from earlier. Especially the backs of my legs."

They curled up in the bed together and talked about the magic that Beau had. Danielle wanted to be able to be a cat, but he had to ask for permission for that. Just as he was dozing off, she reminded him that he had to help his brother Jameson tomorrow, too, with his moving. His house was finished too, and they were all going to help him move into it. He'd opted not to have furniture with his so that he could pick things up as he made his way around.

"Archie has a town meeting tomorrow. He doesn't expect that many people to show up, but I told him that everyone would be there just to make sure that he really was taking over the job." She asked how long he'd been mayor. "About six months now. He was appointed to the job when the FBI was called in to investigate the theft of the money that was earmarked for projects. They found the money, but since it is being used for evidence, it might not get to him anytime soon for him to be able to use it for what it was intended.

Like the new parking lot for the school, not to mention the jail that needs new supplies like guns and vests."

"That sounds like something that needs to be taken care of right away. I mean, what do they do if there is a robbery or something around here?" He told her what he'd been told about how some of the men were using their own guns. "That would be costly. We should do something for the station house that will get them their needs."

"Weston is trying to get the taxes raised again so that they can get at least some of the things that they're running out of. The vests that they have now are really old and are deemed useless." She couldn't believe it and asked what they were going to do when someone sued them for not being prepared. "Just for now, hope that it doesn't happen, I guess. I don't know what I'd do if someone were hurt while on the job. But it looks like they'll be able to get some of the things on the tax money that they have now."

Rolling to his side to hold Danielle, he watched as her eyes fluttered closed. She was asleep in no time, and he continued to watch her. Turning off the light on her side of the bed, by moonlight, he thought about all the things that he wanted to do now that they were in the house as a couple. Before, he'd been putting things off, like going through the barn and the two sheds that were on the property, but he wanted to go through them before it got too cold. They were calling for colder temperatures tomorrow, so he'd better get a move on if he was going to at least start on the barn.

When he got up to go to the bathroom after he realized how tired he was again, he got back into bed only to have Danielle curl herself around him once again. Closing his eyes, he was nearly asleep when he realized he'd forgotten to set an alarm to get up in the morning. Too tired to worry with it, knowing that he'd wake up in time, he went to sleep soundly and didn't bother with getting up again that night.

His cell phone ringing was what brought him out of bed. He had ten minutes to get to the office and knew that he was going to be running behind all day with the way things were going. Glad for taking a shower last night, he was out the door eleven minutes after shutting off his phone. The rain had turned into slush last night, and now he was slipping and sliding all over the place while driving to work.

Fearful for Danielle to drive in the nasty stuff, he called out to her to tell her to be extra careful on the roads. She told him that her appointment was canceled due to the weather, and she was happy for it. Sunny said that she'd come over when things warmed up a bit and help her with the magic that she had. Beau was very happy about that.

By the time he was at the office that they'd all purchased for their businesses with their investments, he was sitting at his desk at twenty minutes after nine.

Late, but with the roads the way that they were, no one was moving around quite that early, so it didn't look like he was going to have anything to worry about. Just moving his brother into his house later that day.

As the day wore on, the mess that had greeted him when he got up dried up and didn't look all that bad when it was time to close up the shop. Weston had come by with Wrangler and Wills, his son, and brought him lunch, so it was a good afternoon. Wills was always a hoot to be around, so he enjoyed talking to him about school. He was a good kid, and everyone was glad to have him as part of the family. By one-thirty, he was on his way home with having a very productive day in getting things squared away about their investments.

Since their father had taught them on the side about investments, the six of them had been doing it without their mother knowing. She didn't want them to have a job that she didn't control, and especially not any money that she didn't give them. So they'd all been investing their money and turning it into millions behind her back. She would have beaten them, no matter how old they were, if they ever did anything that she didn't approve of, or had her dad hire someone to knock them around. It had been difficult living with the two of them, as she wasn't the least bit afraid of them being bigger than her. She'd been a nightmare when they'd been growing up and had caused them all kinds of fights between the six of them to the point that they hated one another. It was a bad time for them until she was killed at the courthouse during her trial for murder with her father.

Danielle was in the kitchen with their cook when he ventured home, and he kissed her on the mouth when he found her. She told him how she was making sure that everyone was working well together now that the faeries had found their own homes in the house and were living there all the time. There were a great many of them in their home, so they had to make sure that they were following the rules that they'd figured out for them.

"We were talking about the freezer and how, since she's been here, Tess has been able to put away some of the things that you can only have in the summer. Like her peach pies and zucchini bread. There are other pies as well as some freezer jam that we can have in the winter months, too, that will be great to have."

"I've been thinking about some homemade bread with soup all day." Pasty told him that was what they were having. Potato cheese soup with homemade bread. "Sounds wonderful. After moving Jameson into his place, it will hit the spot. It's still a little cold out, but not freezing yet. I can't wait until dinner."

Since Jameson said that he wanted to treat them to dinner, they were all going to meet at their house to have soup and bread. It was his favorite kind of soup to have, and the homemade bread was going to be perfect with all the creaminess of the soup. He was going to work extra hard on getting the place moved into so that he could come home and have dinner. At least that was his plan. Who knew what they were going to be running into with a new house on the land.

Chapter 8

Jameson was laughing at himself as the last piece of furniture had been moved in. There was so very little of it in the house that he wondered why he'd even bothered with getting it without stuff he could move in.

But he'd fill it out. Tomorrow, he had an appointment with an estate lawyer to go over the things that had been left over from when his client had died. The other attorney said that he could buy anything that was left after the kids took what they wanted, which turned out to be very little.

"They'd gotten what they wanted in the way of money, and the rest of the treasures were just junk as far as they were concerned. One granddaughter took the desk that had been in the office for decades, but she said that she didn't have any room for anything else to put in her place. Sad when there is so much that gets tossed away because of greed, don't you think?" He agreed with the man, telling him that he'd been picking up things at estate sales for a long time and had them in storage for when he got a house. "Most people don't want houses anymore. They want condos where they don't have to do anything but live there. Someone else to mow the lawn and get the snow off the driveway."

"I honestly love shoveling the driveway when the snow comes in." Thad, the other man, said he was nuts. "I usually get tired of it by the fourth or fifth snow that comes in, but I still make sure that I get it shoveled out. I don't care to have the snow build up on the drive so that I can't get out at any time I want."

"I usually walk to work so that I don't have to mess with a car. Sometimes when it's raining badly, I regret not having one, but usually I can get back and forth to my home before most of the people that I work with can even get out of the parking lot where we work." Jameson agreed that it was a good perk for walking. "You walk too?"

"I do. Especially in the summer months when it's too hot to mess with anything else. I can get in my miles before the end of the week, and that's been a gift I love as well." Thad asked him how much else he'd done to keep in shape. "I run a great deal year-round."

He didn't tell the other man that he and his cat enjoyed running year-round, but he did tell him that he can run at least seven to twelve miles a day when he's out. That was what he was looking forward to the most: having his own place to run around the yard in. He figured that he'd get to run more with his brothers, too, since all their houses were on the same track of land that their father had left them.

Jameson tried to get out with his cat at least five times a week. It made him feel better about himself, not to mention all the exercise that was a benefit from being a shifter. There were lots of perks he thought of being a shifter. Mostly it had to do with feeling himself at least once a day, even if he had to shift in his condo and stretch out. One thing that his father always taught him was never to neglect your cat. It wouldn't do well if he weren't there when you needed him in a hurry.

"You really don't have that much stuff for a house this size." He told his brother Wrangler that he was working on it. "You'd better be working harder, little brother. You're the last one without a mate. I would imagine that she'll be coming along soon now that all of us have one."

"I'm not worried. If she comes before the house is finished, then she can help me fill it out." He told him about the estate that he was going to buy things at next week. "I'm about as ready for her as I can be without actually having her around. Like I said, I'm not worried about her coming around. She'll be here when she gets here."

It took them no time at all to get the house situated. There were things in boxes still left over, but nothing that couldn't be put away by one person. They were all surprised that he had a nice China set that he'd gotten somewhere that had over twenty place settings with it. Including silverware that looked really good with it. Jameson's plan was to wash it all and put it away so that if he ever had them all over, they'd be able to use the dining room set. All he needed to make that happen, however, was a dining room table and chairs.

"Dinner at your house, correct?" Beau said that they were expecting everyone to come over for soup and homemade bread as well as desserts. "I've been looking forward to it all week. Then tomorrow you're going with me to the estate sale. That should be fun for the two of us. Some bonding time together."

"I'm looking forward to it too." They finished up moving the boxes; there did seem to be a great many of them into the rooms that they belonged in. "Mostly it's the company, but I'm starving too, so that'll be nice to have some good food too."

At Beau's home, they were served soup and bread at the magical table. He might have to think about one like this as it stretched out to accommodate all the brothers and their mates with extra chairs. It was wonderful to have them all at the same table and to be able to talk to each other. He missed his family sometimes when it was just the six of them. He might have to get them all together sometimes, when he could, so that they could just be brothers for a time. Not that he didn't love the wives of his family, but he did miss them just being family. Perhaps that would change when he got his own mate to live with him.

Jameson wasn't in a hurry to get a mate. He wanted things to be set up and ready for her when she came around. He knew that there had been a great deal of indecision when Beau and Danielle had decided to live in the house that she already had, and he didn't want that with his own mate. However, he didn't know what would happen if she came along in the next few days, weeks before he had his house finished. Maybe she'd be all right with the flux of the house, but he didn't want that.

After they ate, filled up with the best dinner he'd had in a while, especially one that was homemade, they all sat around the living room talking about the payout on some of the investments that they'd made as a family. While he didn't invest his own money, his brothers made sure that when they hit on a great deal to be had, they'd bring him in on it as well. He was doing all right with his job as a family attorney, but it didn't hurt to have extra money coming in from investments as well.

Then they got to talking about the holidays and how they were fast approaching. In just a little over a month, it would be Halloween, then after that, two short months, and they'd have Thanksgiving and Christmas. Then there would be a whole new year to contend with. He didn't know which holiday he was looking forward to most. But he did love Halloween.

It was the children that he enjoyed the most. The

way they would dress up and go to each house for some well-deserved treats. He never minded the older kids out and doing it either. He had never been allowed to go out trick-or-treating when he'd been younger. Even though there would have been something free for his mother to resell, she never gave out candy either. It had been a great embarrassment for him when he'd been a child not to be able to dress up at school on the day of the holiday. They were just the Sheppard children with the mean mom who never allowed them to do anything that was fun.

They'd never been able to do the trick-or-treating game; their father would sneak them candy for the entire week before and after the holiday. It was the first time in his life that he had ever known that his father had gone against their mother, and it had been a fun way to pull the wool over her eyes. It was fun and scary as hell, too, to know that if she caught them, there would be a beating like no other. But she never did, and their father did it year after year, right up until she killed him. Mother had never liked their father and was surprised daily that she'd ever let him live as long as he had. She'd also killed her own mother, so it was no surprise when Dad ended up dead too.

"What do you know about that woman, Marsha Watson? Since we don't know what her name really is, that's all I've been able to call her." Jameson told Archie what he'd been able to find out. "A game? I doubt that anyone in the Watson family thought that it was a game. Didn't she say that she was their mother from the very start?"

"She's done this to other families, too. One, she claimed that she was the illegitimate daughter of the man, so that they'd pay her off. The couple ended up getting a divorce since the man would never admit to having an affair with someone to have created a child." Beau thought that was just sick. "She's done it before that, too. Pretending to be some long-lost relative that should be part of an estate. The Feds have figured out that she was getting DNA samples from the bodies at the funeral home where she worked. Donald had been right in saying that she was the hairdresser from the funeral home. He'd gotten her scent or something. However, this was the first time that she'd ever been someone who had been dead, like their mother."

"So that's how she made her money by pretending to be someone in their family who would need to be paid off. I'll say it again, that's just sick. How did she think that she was going to be able to get away with it in the Watson's family? I'm assuming the same way." Jameson told Beau that her plan had been—at least that's what the Feds were speculating—to get in good with both families and demand that she have part of their money too. "She never counted on them being jaguars or even shifters when she played her game, as she calls it. She's even trying to get the police to tell her that it should be a law that they tell when people are shifters or not. As you can well imagine, with so many shifters working at the police station, it didn't go over all that well."

They all got a good laugh out of that. And he was glad; things could have been bad had she gotten away with it. Nash even suggested that since she wanted it to be a law, she was planning on doing it once again if she got out.

"Do you think she will?" Jameson said that it was only going to be a matter of time before word got around to those that she'd duped. "I can imagine that they'll want their money back and her to be in prison as well. What do you think about all this, Rogen? It was your family that she tried to take to the cleaners."

"I never wanted to believe that she was our mother. Then, when I found out for sure, it was like she was killed all over again." She looked around the room. "I might not have gotten through it without you guys around to keep me going. I know that the rest of the family is like that as well. Grateful for your support when we found out the truth."

"I can't believe she thought it was just a game and shouldn't be in trouble because of it. I heard that she kept saying that down at the stationhouse. That people need to have a better sense of humor when it comes to having tricks played on them. She also claims that you guys won, so you shouldn't be having her arrested because she was out a great deal of time and money for trying to make this work." Weston shook his head as he continued. "I think that she's crazy and needs to be locked up for every time she tried this scam. It was hurtful and mean, not to mention causing a lot of trouble for that couple about the affair. I'd be pissed off if I were them."

"The Feds are notifying them now. Everyone they know that she tried this on." Archie asked how many people that would be. "Six so far but they're still looking over records at the funeral home. Since it's closed down, the funeral home, I mean, it's been a good deal harder to find people who might have used her as their stylist. That's where she got the DNA from. Before they were embalmed. So, they're thinking that the embalmer or embalmers had something to do with it as well. Whether she paid them off or something along those lines is all they have to go on right now."

"Christ, this is a nightmare more than I thought it was. What does your family have to say about this, Rogen?" She told him. "I can see that. All of you pressing charges is the only way to keep her in jail so that she ends up in prison after the trial. I hope she gets life for all the trouble that she's caused."

"It's doubtful that she'll get life, but she'll be in for a good long time. I'm representing the family when it goes to trail, and there will be other attorneys there that will be representing the other five families that they've uncovered so far." Archie asked him how many they were expecting to be a part of this. "At least a dozen. We're looking into her taking blood from the funeral home, as well as other things that she stole from the bodies of the deceased."

No matter how anyone looked at this, it was going to be the trial of the century. So many things were dependent on the funeral directors' cooperation, and since they'd already had trouble that caused them to be shut down. This was just going to be another bad thing that happened to the place where people would be demanding money for the probability of her taking their families' DNA, too.

~*~

Beau decided that he was going to invest in the little company in his town. The woman made soaps that she was selling on the internet. She needed a loan that would give her space to make more of her product and more equipment to make it happen for her. She'd already shown that she had the sales; it was just having the room and equipment that was keeping her from making the kind of money that she could be making.

Tessa Graham was working from her kitchen in a small apartment. She had some equipment that she was using now, and she had the necessary ingredients to make some more soap. However, without the extra help that she needed to get the sales out there, she was only making enough to cover her expenses and nothing extra.

"I don't know that I want to expand enough to owe you a great deal of money, but my sales are getting better daily, so I have to work through the night. I'd like to be able to sleep for a bit before I get sick." He said that he thought that she should either go big or not do it at all. "I can make seven soaps a day with different fragrances and designs. With the investment of your money, I can do four times that much and still have time to rest when I need it. As it stands right now, I work too long and hard with my other job to be able to keep up."

"You've already shown that you have the right product. With the influx of money, you would be able to have three days to design and make soap, a couple of days to send things out, and you'd still be able to make things work out for you." She thought that the building would be the biggest help. "No doubt. It looks like you're using every available space you have now for drying and curing the soaps. It would be nice if you could have one location in the shop for each step of the process. And you need to hire others to do some of the things that you can shift to them. Like the shipping of the soaps. Or just the cutting."

"I've been doing it all on my own all along. I don't know if I can trust someone else to help me when it comes to cutting the soap." He said she was going to burn out and fail if she didn't get help for the bigger orders she was getting. "I've been approached about having my soaps in a department store, too. I'd love to be able to supply their stores with my stuff."

"Again, you're not going to be able to do that without help. And I would suggest that you also hire yourself an attorney to keep up with your growing company." She nodded, but he could tell that she was still indecisive. It was going to have to be up to her if she could make this work or not. "You let me know what it is you want to do, and I'll be here for you. Whatever you decide will be up to you only."

"I know that I have to make a decision, but I'm afraid that I'll make the wrong one." He thought that everyone was afraid of that who went into business on their own. But he didn't say that to her. "I'll think very hard on it and get back to you. I just need to think about how much it's going to cost me to borrow the money that gets me in debt to make soap. It's just soap and something that I love to do. But I know that I have a decision to make. And I will. Soon."

"Good." He ended the meeting by giving her one of his cards he'd just had printed up. It was Danielle's idea that he have them to hand out, and so far it was working out well for him. As soon as he was in his car, driving back to the office that they all used, he felt good about letting her decide without putting on too much pressure. In the long run, it would be all about her that had to make it work and nothing to do with him.

Once he was in the office, he began looking over the rest of the emails he'd gotten since yesterday. They were people wanting what Tessa had. A hand up in something that they'd been doing or thinking about.

He didn't help them all. Of the three hundred emails that he'd get in a weeks' time he would only help out about one percent of them. He was very careful about how he would take on people whom he would invest in. Mostly, it was advice that he'd give people who asked for help, but sometimes, again, like Tessa, he would see something there that would get him involved. Soap was something that people used every day, and she had some beautiful ideas about what others used to wash their hands with.

Beau was still going through his emails when Danielle called him on his cell phone. She had an idea for dinner and wanted to know how he would like to have pork chops and corn pudding for dinner. He said that it sounded fantastic.

"I was reading one of the magazines in the doctor's office, where I had an interview with, and found a picture of what they were calling comfort food. It sounded really good." He said that he loved comfort food too. "Good. I'll have the cook make it for us. Anything else you'd like to do with it?"

"Cornbread and gravy. Also, some fried apples." She said that her mouth was watering now. "Mine too.

I have about fifty more emails to go through before I look at the investments that we have online. After that, I'll be home. How did the interview go?"

"I got the job. It's just going to be part-time, all I really wanted to do, but I'll be calling people to confirm their appointments, as well as a little bit of filing. He has someone to do most of the filing, but I'd be doing it between patients for him. His office is really small, but he does have a lot of patients coming in all the time. While I was there, I swear he saw a dozen patients between interviewing me. I guess that's why when I was told about the interview, they said that it would take a while. I think I'm going to love working there with him and the other staff members."

"Good. I've known Doctor Benton for a long time. He never approved of the way our mother was treating us when we were brought in, but he didn't do much in the way of helping us. Which I can understand. He'd been trying to get his practice up and running, and Mother was a threat to everyone that he saw. I don't blame him at all for not taking a stand when he could have." She asked him if he minded her working for him. "No, not at all. He's a good man and a great doctor. I just think that he could have done more for us as kids than he did. That's all."

"It's only part-time, which, as I said, is all I wanted, but I'm looking forward to having something to do while you're working." He told Danielle that he understood completely. "Good. If you want to not to work…well, I'm sure that I have to work. I'd go crazy if I didn't. I think you understand that as well."

"I do. Even coming to the office when I can read my emails from home makes me feel like I'm doing something productive." She told him that she felt the same way. "I knew that you'd understand. You're the best thing that could have happened to me."

"I love you too. And I love the way that you make me feel when I'm around you." They talked about her new job, and then she asked about Tessa. "I've used her soap before. It's so pretty that you sometimes feel guilty for messing around with it to use. And the scent that I have, lavender, is the best-smelling soap that I have had in a long time."

"I'm hoping she comes to the decision that will make her more profit. It'll be totally up to her, however."

He told her about some other investments that he'd made today, but mostly it was the advice that he'd give them for free that people used most of the time. He had a knack for helping people by giving them advice when he didn't want to invest with monetary funds.

"I didn't realize that you had so many investments that were ongoing right now." He said that he was forever looking for the next great one that would put someone on the map and make him a great deal of money. "I don't know that I could do that job. I'd be lending out money for every little project because I could. I guess you'd have to be good at reading people to be able to do that."

"Sometimes people are hard-pressed to explain what they want in the way of money and to tell you what they really want to use it for. I've been caught a couple of times with fraudulent investment ideas. I'm more careful now, but still have someone slip under my radar." She told him that she doubted that it happened all that often to him. "You'd be surprised. Sometimes I have to cut my losses, as there is no more money to get from them. That hurts badly. But I will get my money back if I can through any way possible. Even if I have to take their homes. I'm not above suing people for everything they got either if they fuck with me."

"I bet you can be ruthless. I'm glad I'm on your side of this." They both laughed, and it felt good. He loved his mate more than anything that he had. "I need to get off here and let you get some work done so that you can come home on time."

"All right. I'll talk to you tonight." He put his cell phone back in his pocket and continued to look at the emails that he had just gotten. He honestly didn't know where people were getting his email address, but was glad that it was out there. There was no telling what sort of trouble he would be getting into if not for a job like this one. While being able to come and go as he pleased, he stuck to a schedule so that he wouldn't miss work. It was either that or, like he'd said to Danielle, he'd be getting himself into all kinds of trouble letting his mind wander around like it was prone to do.

After closing down his computer, he sat and talked to his brother Weston for a little bit. He was going over some of the things that he had going on as mayor of their city. He asked him if he was going to run for the next election or if he had had enough of cleaning up the mess of someone else.

"I'm going to run. I've enjoyed being able to help out the little town we live in. Especially since I never thought that I'd be able to do anything for it when Mother was alive. While I didn't expect her to die so young, she was only in her late fifties, as you know, I thought that she'd be around forever keeping us in line." Beau said he tried hard not to think about her anymore. "I do a great deal. When I have a decision to make, I wonder what she would say about it and do the exact opposite. It usually turns out to be a good decision."

That made him burst out laughing with his brother. "I can see you totally doing that, too. So when a big decision comes up from now on, I'm going to do the same thing. Think about what Mother would have done and do the opposite. Yes, I love that."

"It might not be the way to go all the time. You understand that, don't you?" He said that he did and wouldn't do it if it still felt wrong. "Good for you.

I've been thinking of ways that we can get some of the townspeople off our backs about how we treated mother and grandfather. I say we get them both a really nice headstone. One that is over their heads so that we know they're not coming back from the dead."

"They have a headstone. It just says their names and their date of birth and death on it." Weston said he knew that, but wanted something bigger and better. "I don't know about that. People might think that we've changed our minds about them and have come to respect them."

"I thought of that too, but it's just us that would know differently." He told Weston that it sounded like more trouble than it was worth. Just to get a few townspeople off their backs. "It was just a thought. I'm sick of dealing with them. I think of all of us, I'm the one who has to be around them the most. Daily, I get people coming in here who tell me that I should have treated them better or been a better son. I know what they were like, and while they might not, it's getting on my last nerve to have to deal with them."

"I'm sorry that you have to deal with anyone who thinks that our mother was as saintly as they think she was. And grandfather too. He would beat us every day if Mom wanted him to. But the very fact that he killed Dad and Grandma is what I can't get with people treating us as badly as they do. It came out in the newspaper that they both killed them off, and they

still think of her as this nice person." Weston said that
he gets that, too. "They act like the newspaper got it all
wrong about her, and we're just paying people to say
bad things about her. If they only knew."

"You know, talking to you has opened my eyes,
so to speak. I don't want anything to do with making
people believe better of me. I know what happened, as
you said, and if people can't get over that, then that's
all on them. Yes, you're right in not getting them a
bigger headstone just so people will leave me alone.
I'm sorry that I brought it up." Beau said he was sorry
that he had to deal with them. "I am as well, but I'm
doing something now that makes me feel better, and
the rest of the people who think I'm a bad son can fuck
off."

On his way home, he thought about what
Weston had said about their mother and grandfather,
and he felt bad that some of the townspeople were still
acting like they did nothing wrong. They'd murdered
people around the town to the point they were going
to prison for a very long time, if not for life. People
should remember that about them, too.

Chapter 9

Danielle loved her job, but she loved being able to hang out with people that she didn't know all that well better. They did gossip a great deal and had comments about everyone that came in—sometimes good, sometimes bad. But they were a close-knit group of people that she thought could be funny at times. Also, she was getting useful information about people and how they needed help when they did.

"Did you hear about the Singer family? They had to sell part of their farm when the taxes came due again. If they keep chopping it up like that, there won't be enough ground for those kids to play on come summer." She made a mental note to ask Beau if he could help them in some way. However, she knew that if he did that, then he'd be helping the entire town out of jams when they needed help. "Mr. Singer is going out for one of those jobs out in the ocean on a rig. I don't know that I could do that, being so far from my family all the time."

"I heard that they're on for six weeks and off for six weeks. That wouldn't be so bad." One of the nurses decided that there might be fewer Singer children if he were gone for a while. "I can see that too. Aren't there like ten of them now?"

"There are only four of them, and they're getting to be school age now. Must be a relief to the mother if that's what's going on." She tuned them out for calling several people on the phone to remind them of their upcoming appointments. When she got off, they were onto another family.

"I've seen her in town buying groceries. I don't know how she feeds them all on what little he makes, but she must do all right. They all seem healthy enough when she brings them in for checkups and such." One of the receptionists said that she doesn't buy things that are premade either. "I heard tell they have a garden that is as big as their yard and that the kids all work in it with her while the mister is working. Must be nice to get your kids to do anything that you tell them. I can't even get my teenage son to make his bed, and it's a sleeping bag."

She didn't know who they were talking about, but she knew that a lot of the staff here had children who were less than helpful around the house. And getting them to pick up after themselves had caused more than one argument, too. She wondered what Beau would think of her making the kids clean up after themselves and thought that he'd be just fine with it. He cleaned up after himself when he was home with her.

As she made her next round of calls, she kept an ear out for anything that sounded dangerous. She'd already heard about one of them carrying a gun to church—just in case. In case what scared her a bit, but since she didn't go to the same church as she did, she felt marginally safer.

Danielle didn't join in their gossip but only listened to it. She knew a great deal about the doctor, too, that she was sure he'd be upset about if he knew. They weren't vicious about their gossip, but they told what they had learned from talking to the people who came in and said to them.

She also knew about the previous mayor, too, and why Weston had taken over the job when he'd been run out of town. He and his wife had been arrested, finally, and were awaiting their trial like a few other people were. They'd had their funds frozen and their homes overseas taken from them in order to get the money back that they'd stolen from the town. That's what Weston was dealing with right now. Lack of funds to get things done that should have been done ages ago.

"Do you suppose they'll get away with it?" She must have missed something while on the phone and decided the next call could wait. "I mean, it is mail fraud if nothing else. And once the Feds are involved with it, there'll be no hiding from them either."

"Is it mail fraud? I mean, I know that they're

mailing the stuff through the postal service, but is that really what's involved? Couldn't they just be getting in trouble for selling the drugs to someone out of state?" A nurse said that it was mail fraud. "Oh well, I didn't know if they'd get them on that. I hope they're caught soon. It bothers me that they're selling drugs through the mail. It could be going to anyone in town, and we'd never know about it."

"I was thinking about giving an anonymous tip. But I'm fearful that it'll come back and bite me in the ass, and they'll be getting out soon. Just what I need is for them to find out that I had turned them in." She wanted to ask about what and who, but the phone was ringing again and she had to answer it.

The woman on the phone wanted to be able to come into the office at five-thirty. They closed up shop around here at four, and she couldn't make her understand that. She said it would only take one nurse and the doctor to see her, and that shouldn't be such a big deal. Well, it was a big deal to hold the offices open for an hour and a half for one person.

"You just tell him who it is, and I'll bet he'll say that it's no trouble. You ask him and I'll wait." She said that he was a very busy man and she wasn't going to ask him about that. "You're just being a bitch. When I tell him how I was treated, then you'll lose your job. Can it be worth losing your job because of one stupid appointment at five-thirty?"

"The problem is, as I've stated to you already, that the offices close at four and that appointment you want is an hour and a half later than we're open. No one is going to want to stay after all that time when they could be at home with their families. I'm not going to put you down for that time because we're closed." Then she hung up the phone. The women in the office with her applauded her.

"We've been dealing with her for years and years about having a special time for coming in. You not only didn't take her shit, but you got to hang up on her too. She usually hangs up on us first." The phone rang again, and they said it was going to be her. "She's thinking that if she calls back in, she'll get someone else. But you go ahead and answer it. It'll piss her off."

"Dresden Doctors' offices, how may I help you?" It was her again, and she was going on with the same things that she'd used before. That the doctor would be upset about her not getting to see him when she could. After about twenty seconds of her going on about the doctor, she must have realized that it was Danielle again and started cursing. Danielle just simply hung up the phone and smiled at her coworkers. "I hope I don't lose my job over this. I like working here."

They all got a big laugh out of it. So much so that the doctor came to find out what was so funny. After being told who it was, he didn't even have to hear the reason she'd been hung up on; he knew from past calls.

"You're right in saying that I don't want to wait around for her to come in. I have enough going on with my regular hours. And the one time that I did give in and give her the appointment, she didn't show up, telling me that she had other things come up and couldn't make it." He shook his head. "Never again. To anyone else, for that matter, will I stay over for a patient unless it's an emergency. And it had better be one too, or they'll be without a doctor."

The rest of the afternoon went well. They never mentioned the mail fraud case again, and she was all right with that. They would, and she'd be prepared for it. After today, she'd be more of a participant when it came to their gossip and find out as much as she could about anyone who needed their help. She was going to look into the Singer family, too, just to make sure that things were all right for the family.

When the office closed up at four, she was out the door by ten after. Everyone was going to meet at the local pizza shop and enjoy a beer after work. She'd been invited too and was going to go enjoy some time with them. Besides, Beau had to work late, and she knew that he'd not be home until well after seven o'clock. She knew that she'd be home in plenty of time before he was.

"You're married to one of the Sheppard men, aren't you?" Nurse Sacaton, Deb, was asked to call her asked what it was like to be married to someone that wealthy. "I mean, I was wondering why you're even working, being married to one of them."

"I don't want to be a stay-at-home housewife. I would go crazy with nothing to do all day." She said she'd love to be able to stay at home all day. She'd make a good time of it. "I tried it for a while, but it's really not for me. I would imagine that it would be great for some people, but not for me. I need to get out and be around people."

"I guess I can see that. But I'd be hard-pressed not to want to stay at home all the time. I don't know about when children would come along." They all had their opinion about what they'd do if they were a stay-at-home mom. "My husband wants me to get pregnant soon, and I'm not so sure. If he had a steady job, then maybe, but right now I'm the breadwinner in the family and the one who cooks the bread when we're hungry. I don't see it working out with us having a kid. Even though he said he'd stay at home with it, I don't see that happening either. He'd be complaining about that too."

She felt sorry for Deb when the other women teased her about having a deadbeat husband. Then they asked her if she'd been beaten anymore, and she felt more sorry for her than before. It would be terrible to be beaten by someone who was supposed to love you for all time. Then the other women talked about how they'd been knocked around by their husbands, too. She didn't know what to say to them about that.

"Couldn't you just leave him?" And go where they asked. "I don't know, but staying with a man who knocks you around doesn't seem all that safe either. How do you put up with that?"

"My mom was an abused wife, I think my grannie was as well. It's what most men to do women who work outside the home when they can't hold down a job." She asked why they couldn't hold down something as simple as a job. "For many reasons, I guess. They blame it on us, too, for us being ashamed of them. I'm ashamed of myself for not being able to get away from him. And it's not like we want to be millionaires like your family is, but it would be nice if they were to have a job that paid well. Anything at this point."

"I'm sorry, but I don't think that I could stand a man beating on me all the time because he can't hold down a job." One of the others said it was something that you get used to. "I don't think so. It would be harder to leave, I'm sure, if there are children involved, but none of you have children, so I don't understand how you could stay with him."

"I don't know either, but as I said, you get used to it." Danielle didn't even want to work with the women anymore if they were going to allow someone to beat on them when they had a good job making enough money to support themselves in anything that they wanted to do. "He can be all right when he's not drinking. I look forward to those days more than ever. Someday, he'll hit me too hard, and that will be the end of him. That's all I can say about it."

After heading home after leaving the bar, she decided that she wasn't going to continue to stress the importance of leaving an abusive relationship like the ones that they were in. Also, she'd try her best to get information from them about the mail fraud. These women were good people, just in trouble with their spouses.

She was surprised to find Beau home when she got there. He told her that his meeting had been canceled, but he was glad that she'd been out with friends. She told him what she'd found out during her shift, and he was concerned about the mail fraud like she was. He asked her some questions, and since she didn't know, he said that he'd ask Sunny to look into it. She had a way about her that could get to the bottom of things faster than anyone he knew.

"Because she's magical?" Beau told her that it was, and her mother was as well. "Well, I hope she can take care of this. Whoever it is has been selling things to people for some time now, and it could be kids around here."

~*~

It had taken Sunny's mom to help with finding out

who was selling the drugs. Lucky for them, he lived right here in town and was caught with the goods not a week later. Tomorrow, the judge was in town, so there was going to be a hearing for both him and his little crew, plus Allison Dale, otherwise known as Marsha Watson.

"Is she still claiming that it was a game?" Beau couldn't believe it either, but didn't have much to do with the woman or the trial that was going to be coming up. It would only be a hearing to find out if there was enough evidence to hold her over for trial or not, but he'd seen some of the material that his brother had, and he thought it would be more than enough to hold her. "I heard that she's giving the officers at the stationhouse a lot of trouble, too. I hope she gets the book thrown at her."

"I'm not holding out any hope of it getting much in the way of sentencing. She's off her rocker if you were to ask me. And she's decided that since it was only a game she was playing against the Watson family, then she should be able to get out on good behavior. Which, from my understanding, isn't something to count on." Beau asked about her trial and when he thought it would be, if there was one. "I'm thinking that it's going to be sometime next summer. That will give both attorneys time to gather up what is needed and see to her prison term. There is no doubt that she'll go to prison, but it's the question of how long that bothers me. I hope she at least gets ten years. Perhaps that will make her less likely to do this sort of thing again."

"I don't want to be rude, but is there anything else we can talk about other than this woman?" Beau asked Weston what he meant. "It seems as if we talk about her endlessly. There has to be other people around town that we can talk about. Even if it's just our family. She's not all that special if you ask me."

"No, she's not, and you're right. Let's talk about how we're going to have gardens put in next year for whoever wants one." That was a good topic, he thought, and was glad that someone brought it up.

Come spring, they were going to have raised gardens for any citizen who wanted one. It would be something that they could plant whatever they wanted in it and harvest it for their own tables. The gardens would be free to the public, but they had to be maintained so that they would not be an eyesore if they were to get out of hand. Beau was especially happy about the project as he loved cooking with fresh vegetables and herbs. He'd already heard from two people about their new gardens and how they were going to grow pumpkins in the fall to sell around town. He thought that was a great idea as he loved pumpkin pie.

"We're getting the soil at a good discount that we're going to be using. And the greenhouse just outside of town is going to offer a discount on their plants for those who buy from them. Also, I don't know if you know this or not, but the local hardware store is also offering a discount on tools they can use as well." Beau asked if everyone had signed up for the gardens or not. "All the places that we were going to put in have been claimed. If we had twice as many to get out, we'd have them taken as well. I think it's going to be a huge hit with the locals."

"Ms. Tanner said she's going to put her things out early enough that she can have a second season. I don't know how that would work, but she's excited about it. I've also heard that some of the people are sharing the workload, too. I know that it can be hard on the elderly to get out there every day and work on the garden." Beau said that some of the pack was going to help them out by weeding for them when it's too hot for them. "Good job. That'll be great for them. Especially some of the older groups that have gotten one of the gardens."

They spoke about the gardens until lunch time and then changed the subject to getting ready for Halloween. The courthouse was going to be handing out candy, with Weston and Rogen there to hand it out. Then there was Jameson's law office, too, going to hand out the big kind of candy bars that the kids loved. It seemed to him that the town was going all out this year, and he couldn't be more proud of them. He and Danielle were going to be handing out candy, too, at their home with the faeries. They were excited about being around the children, too.

They'd already gotten lots of bags of candy since they were situated right off the main road going through town. He'd been telling kids that they were going to be disappointed if they didn't see some of the kids at their home, too. Beau thought that this was going to be the best holiday ever.

~*~

The faeries were going to help her with her costume for trick-or-treat night. Danielle was happy to have them with her and Beau as part of their costumes. Beau was going to dress up as a faerie lord, and she was going to be a faerie princess. They'd been planning it all month so that the faeries could be a part of the night. They were going to be flying around like part of the show.

"Do you suppose we could give a little magic to some of the children?" She asked Stack what he meant. "Just to ones that seem to be needing a little extra loving and friendship. It would only be a spark that would last through the night. Then it would be gone the next day. But it might give them what they need in order to be brave about becoming friends with some of the other children."

"I don't see a problem with it so long as it's not dangerous. Nor does it last that long. We don't want to harm the children in any way." Stack said he'd never do that but would like to see the children happy. "You know, parents go all out on this holiday as well. Some of them work really hard on costumes for their kids, too. They might need a little boost from you as well."

"Oh, how exciting for us." Stack was going to rotate all the faeries that wanted to be a part of it throughout the night. It might only be for a few minutes, but with the number of kids in their town, they might well get to see a lot of children. She'd heard from them that they get a special kind of magic from children that they can't get anywhere else.

The faeries had been very helpful since they got the house finished. She still felt bad for not allowing them to do the house when she first moved in with Beau. It would have saved her a great deal of time and heartache. Going through the things that had been left behind by her father had been hard, but things from her grandmother had really killed any kind of love for the woman. She was a mean, nasty sort of person that had ruled them all with an iron fist. Even when they were adults.

She was setting the table when Beau came home from work. In the morning, they were going to the courthouse to find out what happened with the two people they had an interest in. The other Sheppards were going to be there as well because they were going to support Rogen and the rest of the Watson family. Jameson was going to be their attorney, and she thought that he was looking forward to that as much as they were getting things done with the other woman. She'd caused enough trouble as it was.

"What are we having?" She told him. "I love pot roast and potatoes. Especially with bread to sop up the gravy with. How was work today?"

"Better. I think that I'm getting used to their gossip and can tune it out better. I don't mind that they say things anymore about people, but I wish they'd stop it. Some of the things they say are just plain mean." He agreed with her but never asked what they were saying. She'd tell him if it involved something that they could do something about. But usually, he would only hear about it if she mentioned it in passing. "Did I tell you that tomorrow is my day off? I'm going to the library to read to the younger kids at noon."

"I wanted to do that when we were younger, but Mother wouldn't allow us to be associated with those sorts of people. She treated us with disdain when we even mentioned it."

Beau had told her the other night about how his grandfather had beaten him so badly that he had three broken ribs as well as a bloodied lip. He wasn't allowed to shift either to make himself better. It was his punishment for asking if he could get a job after school in his junior year. While he did heal faster than a human would, it was still several weeks before he could get around without wincing. "I don't miss them at all. Not even when I'm down in the dumps about something do I think about them in a good way. I'm not glad that they're dead, I wish they could have gone to prison for some time for what they did, but I'm happy that they're not in my life."

Danielle couldn't believe how well they turned out for what had been done to them as children through their adult years. She didn't think she could have survived had she even had half of the way they'd been treated. But each one of them was kind and well-mannered. They treated their fellow man the same way they treated everyone, with compassion and tenderness. Sometimes they could be harsh when the time called for it, but otherwise they were the nicest men that she knew.

After dinner, they stayed in the dining room just talking about their day. Beau had several investments of his own that he was keeping an eye on, and he was happy to report that the woman he'd been trying to get to expand, Tess the soap woman, was going to take him up on his offer to help her so that she could get into a bigger building and make a name for herself. Jameson was going to go over the contracts with her next week, and that would be the beginning of a whole new relationship.

"She'll be making the kind of money that she only dreamed of once she gets up and going. It's going to take about a month to get all the equipment that she needs in place, but after that she'll be rolling along."

She asked if she was going to make other kinds of soaps. "Not at first. She just wants to get her product out in a timely manner so that she can get some reviews from people who bought from her."

"Well, I'm happy for her. You said that the building that you're getting for her would have a shop where she could sell things too. I'm going to make it a point to go there weekly to make sure I don't miss any of her new designs or smells." He said with a laugh that she should work for her. "I thought about it. But I was worried that she'd think I was spying on her for you. I don't want her to think that when you guys have a good relationship going on right now."

"I guess that's true. I'd hate for her to feel obligated too in thinking that she'd have to hire you. You're brilliant, have I told you that?" She told him not enough, and they both laughed. "Anyway, I've been reaching out to other vendors that I've come across when we're out and about. Did you know that there is a quilting club in town? They make the most beautiful quilts I've ever seen. And they usually donate them to causes so that they can be raffled off. That's where the one they're working on now goes to the Center for Adults. I guess they need new books in their library, and this is a good way to make the money to purchase them."

"The town library has had a raffle too. They get money from late fees and such, but sometimes they need to have whole sections replaced. The children's area is in such a state of flux all the time that I'm surprised when they have raffles and fundraisers that get them money enough to buy whole sections of books." He asked her if they take donations; it seemed like a good cause to donate to. "Yes, they do. I don't know the address right now, but I can get it for you tomorrow. I'm excited to be a part of the library where people can go to use the computers and books at the same time."

After locking up the house, they were headed to bed. Danielle was exhausted and needed about fifty hours of sleep, but knew that she'd not miss a night making love with Beau for anything. However, almost as soon as her head hit her pillow, she was out for the night. She woke up briefly when Beau wrapped himself around her, but then she went right back to sleep. It would be good to get a full night's rest when she had so much to do tomorrow.

Chapter 10

On cross-examination, Jameson seemed to be getting answers to questions that he didn't ask. Every time he brought up the 'game' that Allison had been playing, she'd go on this tirade about how nobody should be upset with her for having some fun. Even bringing up that no one had had any fun with her supposed game, she still didn't understand why she'd been jailed when the Watsons had won.

"Won what?" She could never get past the fact that she thought what she was doing was just fine, as she'd not hurt anyone nor had anyone died. "But they did have to relive the death of their mother over again when you thought to tease them into thinking that she was still alive. Most family members were upset with you because of the way that you treated them. Lying to them about their mother."

"It's just something that I do. I can't believe that anyone would believe that I was their long-dead mother anyway. That's what makes it so much fun for me. To see who breaks down first. Usually it's the oldest children, but this time I couldn't fool any of them. That's how they won against a professional like myself." He asked her where she got the DNA from that said she was their mother. "I didn't use it, so you can't bring that up. But it was easy enough to get when you grease a few palms. Do people still say that? Greasing a few palms? Anyway, that's what I did when I was preparing for this game. There's a great deal of work on my end to make this work. Not to mention money. I had to have my hair dyed a certain color. Boy, was that hard. And have a tattoo — that caused harm to my person getting that done, but am I suing them for that? No, I'm not. I'm just saying that they won, and they should be happy that I've given up so soon. I just don't understand these people."

"Perhaps it's you that they don't understand." She waved him off. She'd done that several times since he'd been talking to her. "I don't understand what that means when you wave me off. Are you admitting that you were wrong to do this? Or are you saying that it doesn't matter how they feel because you've declared them the winner? Of what we still don't know, but there you have it."

"Of course, I'm not going to admit to being wrong about this. I wasn't. They were just more stubborn about listening to me. You know, I had an entire life I was building up just for them. I had things all worked out on how I didn't remember certain things. It was going to be because of a head injury that I had when I was in the accident." He told her that she'd not been in an accident. "You're stupid, aren't you? Not myself, but their mother had been in one. Will you please pay attention?" He only looked at the judge.

"You're going to keep your opinions to yourself about the attorneys. I've told you this before. Just answer the questions they have, then we can get out of here in a reasonable time." There were times when he wanted to shake the shit out of her. But when he'd gotten nothing from her, he sat down. She wasn't going to get away with this, and he was going to do his damnedest to make sure that she ended up in prison for a while. "Mr. Toddler, it's your turn to ask questions. Though I don't know what you're going to expect from her. Mr. Sheppard has been trying for the last several hours."

As Toddler asked about the time she pretended to be a long-lost daughter of a couple, he turned them off. He knew that it was going to be more of the same, and he was frankly sick of dealing with her. But he would simply to get her off the streets and out of the way of trying this again.

"You did really well." He smiled at Rogen when she reached out to him. *"We all knew she was off her noodle, but she's proven that her noodle was wet and without substance, too."*

"If she asks the judge about making this all go away one more time, I think he's going to hit her with his gavel. She seems to have a one-track mind about everything. I wish

I could have gotten her to state the rules of her game, but all she did was wave me off again. I wonder what that means in her mind." Rogen said that she probably made up the rules as she went along. Thus making it impossible for her to tell anyone what they were. "*I can see that. She's been playing this game for the last twelve years, and I don't see her ending it just because she's been caught this time. The rules will change again, and there won't be any more winners as far as she is concerned.*"

"*That's what scares me. She's going to go to some family that is desperate for their family member to be alive and hurt one of them badly, and they'll take it out on her.*" Rogen said that she could only hope that happened. "*I know what you mean. But it won't stop her. Not until she's someplace where she can't get to others to hurt.*"

He heard his name being called out, and he looked up at the judge. He was asking each of the attorneys who were on his side of the room if they wanted to take a break. That he needed one badly. He'd not realized that it was nearly noon when he sat down and agreed that he could use a break as well.

Once he was out of the stuffy building, he drew in a deep breath of air. It had been raining this morning, and now the sun was out and shining brightly. Fall was fast approaching, and he couldn't wait for the cooler weather. It was his favorite time of the year.

"How did the estate sale go?" He grinned at his brother, Nash. "That good, huh? I'm happy for you. I'll help you move it in when you get it here. You did buy enough to fill out more of your home, didn't you?"

"I bought it all. Even the little salt wells that she had in her China cabinet. He made me an offer I couldn't refuse. I even have glasses and silverware that I didn't think that I'd get when I went up there." Nash patted him on the back. "It's being packed up as we speak and brought here over the weekend. The delivery company is even giving me a good deal on bringing it to me because they have another load to take back from here. It saved them money by having a return trip."

"What kind of things did you get? Besides silverware and salt wells?" He told him about the bedroom suits that he got, as well as the records that came with the stereo. He had a list of things that he couldn't believe that he'd gotten for so little money. "You sound like you had fun too."

"I did. The only thing that I didn't buy was the car. It wasn't anything that I could see myself driving around in, so I declined the offer to purchase it." He told him what it was, and Nash agreed that it would be out of place in a town like the one they lived in. "Yeah, expensive cars would have made me stick out like a thumb with a pie on it. Remember when grandma used to say that?"

"I've been thinking about her a lot lately. Her and Dad. I think that he'd be proud of us all with how we've made something of ourselves with what he left us." Jameson didn't remember his dad all that well. He'd been only seven when he'd been killed over twenty years ago now. "I forget about that, too. That you were so young when he was murdered."

"Do you ever wonder what would have happened to us had he not been killed? I mean, do you think that he would have divorced Mother given the chance?" Nash told him that he didn't think their dad had much of a backbone when it came to standing up to Mother. "Yeah, that's what I thought too. I just wondered if he would have taken us away from her and we'd be better off with him."

"I don't think he would have been able to. She was a strong force, as you know. I think that even if he had not been killed when he had, if he'd tried to divorce her, she would have killed him then. She was forever in control of everything that went on." Nash patted him on the back again. "I'm proud of you for how you turned out. I never thought that you'd make it through school with the way that Mother treated all of us. Grandfather didn't help either. I still have the scar that he gave me when I was twelve and asked about dinner being put on the table. He used one of the silverware that was on the table on my arm and stabbed me four times before Archie got him off me."

"I remember that. I thought you were going to bleed to death before you could shift and take care of it." Nash nodded and ordered his lunch for him when they finally made it in line at the ice cream shop. "They make a good burger here, and I'd gladly eat three of them myself. But I don't want to be too full when I have to go back in. I might fall asleep."

The two of them had a good lunch and were joined by the rest of the family. They talked about anything but the trial, and he was glad for that. His mind was working hard enough without adding their opinions to his already overworked mind. And the way things were going, it was going to be a long day, too.

"I have to leave. I have some things to do today." He kissed Danielle on the cheek and told her that he loved her when she made her way to the library. Beau was lucky in his mate because, of all the women, he thought she was the nicest. She sure could make him feel good when he was down in the dumps.

When it was time to go back into the courtroom, he noticed that Allison was missing. Apparently, she'd caused some trouble with the judge and had been sent back to jail for the duration of the day. Thankfully for him, he'd gotten his questions out of the way before she'd left. He didn't know what the others were going to do.

As it turned out, they had plenty of evidence to turn over to the court system and witness statements, too. He was impressed with the others who were sharing the table against the woman and told them so when he had the chance. They were impressed with him because he'd shown her true colors when asking her about her 'game' that she'd been playing. By four-thirty, they were closing up for the day, and he was going to have to come back in tomorrow. He had to admit that it went much smoother with Allison gone.

He and the other lawyers went out for pizza after gathering up their things. He liked them and was glad that they all had a common goal to get Allison off the streets. David said that he had been working on this since she'd approached his client about being his daughter from a previous relationship.

"They divorced soon after. But now that it's coming out about how she tricked them into paying her an ungodly sum of money, they'll be working together to get her to stay in prison. I'd like to know what she's done with all her illegal gains from these scams she's been playing. I mean, so far as I know, she was able to net nearly ten million dollars from other people that she scammed as well."

"That's a great deal of money. I wonder how much she would have gotten from my family had they believed her." David told him that he thought that she was in for the long run with the Watson/Sheppard families. She would have taken them for more money than she had previously gotten all together. "There were things going on that she didn't have any idea about when she came to this town."

"You mean because of the family being shifters? Yeah, I wondered how she was going to make that work out when I read your reports on it. She claimed to be their mother, yet she wasn't a shifter like them. That's another thing that she's been complaining about. That shifters should have to tell people what they are. That it should be the law. The woman is nuts if you were to ask me." Jameson agreed with him. "It's too bad you didn't allow her to get in deeper with herself. She might well have turned and run. But then she'd be doing this to someone else, and they might not have faired as well as you guys did."

That night, when he was at his home, he went over his notes again and decided that he'd had enough. Going into one of the bedrooms he was using as a sorting room, he looked over some of the things that he'd brought back with him the other day. He was just sorting through the linens that he'd gotten when his doorbell rang.

He'd not been expecting company, nor had his family told him that they were coming over, so he didn't know what to expect. Opening the door, there was no one there until he looked at the big truck that was in his driveway. The person coming toward him was saying how she'd gotten things packed up earlier than she thought and had them on the truck.

"It's a lot of the bigger stuff." He asked her what

she was talking about. "The estate manager was able to get all the bigger stuff loaded early and told me to bring it to you. He said that he'd contact you to let you know."

"No one contacted me about anything." He looked into the deep cavern of the back end of the semi and whistled. "There is a lot of stuff on this thing. I'll have to get some help, or you'll have to wait until the weekend. I had no idea you were coming."

"I can't wait for the weekend. I have a load that goes back in the morning." She pulled out her cell phone and made a call. "I'll call now to see what's going on. Can you please make arrangements to have this emptied out tonight?"

He contacted his brothers and asked for their help. They were willing to come over, but he didn't know what he'd do if they hadn't been able to help him. As it was, he was going to have to pay for pizzas, their payment for helping unload everything tonight. It was going to be late, too, for as much stuff that looked like it was in the semi.

~*~

Demi didn't know what to think about the men who were unloading the truck. They didn't even seem mad because the truck was a few days early. But got right to work and unloaded the furniture right off as if it didn't weigh hundreds of pounds. Even things that took four men to load on the other end didn't seem to bother the two men who pulled it off and into the house. And what a house it was, too.

The front hall had been a staging area for some of the things that had come on the truck. She knew they were getting the bedroom things upstairs first and then the living room things last. There were six bedrooms in the house, and enough furniture to make sure that someone could easily sleep in the rooms once they were set up. The linens and other things that she'd seen at the other house were being packed up to come on another smaller truck than the one that she was driving.

"Do I know you?" She'd been asked that before. Not tonight, but by other men hitting on her. She knew that she was good-looking. She kept herself in shape, too. But this man seemed sincere about asking the question, and she was sad to say that she wished she'd known him, but didn't. "You look like someone I've worked with before. Perhaps gone to college with or something."

"The only time I've been on campus is delivering something to them. I did go to college online, but I'm sure that doesn't count." He said that it did as she was getting an education. And then he smiled at her. "You could put the electric company out of business with a smile like that. I'm not hitting on you, but you're a good-looking man."

"Thanks." He moved on when she did, and

they got two more bedroom sets out of the truck. She didn't know who loaded it for her, but they put all the furniture that went together near the other things that went in the same room.

There was no doubt that they were all related. The man that she'd met first seemed to be the baby of the family, and they treated him like it. She'd be pissed off if someone treated her the way that he was being treated, but he seemed to not take them all that seriously. She was glad. It might have been a big fight had they started something with all the work that needed to be done. She looked up when someone said her name. She'd not even realized she'd given it to them, but then remembered it was on the paperwork.

"It says here that there are two more trucks coming to my house. I'm sorry, but it looks to me like I've gotten most of the furniture that I had bought. What other kind of stuff will be on another semi?" She told him that she didn't know that her company had been called in to deliver it and that they said she had a load going back the same way. "I don't know what that means, but that's all right. I guess I'll just have to wait and see."

He stood there staring at her for several long, tense moments before he looked at his family. Then, when she thought that he'd walk away, he took a step toward her and inhaled deeply. Like he was trying to smell her for some reason. She asked him what the hell was going on.

"Nothing. I mean, there is a lot going on, but it's nothing right now. It could be, but right now I'm not going to say anything. I'm not sure that I have it right, so I'm not sure what to say to you right now. It might be a joke that my brothers are playing on me, but then I don't know why they'd do that. Do you? But it could be—" She smacked him when it looked like he was going to continue speaking like he was. He put his hand on his cheek and stared at her. "You're not supposed to be able to cause me any harm."

"You're off your rocker. What the hell are you talking about?" He said she was his mate. "I don't want to be your friend. Or mate, whatever you want to call it. I think you have something wrong with you."

"So do I right now." He moved a step back from her when she lifted her hand to smack him again. "I'm sorry. I'm not making any sense to myself right now. My name is Jameson Sheppard, as you know. You're Demi Rothchild. I didn't mean friend when I said you were my mate, but my mate. Like someone who is supposed to be my everything."

"You've enough shit going on right now without me being your everything. And if you mean what I think you mean, you can just forget about that, too. I don't have time for a husband of sorts, nor do I want one. I have my life just the way I like it." He said that he did as well. "Well, good for you and me. We don't have to take this any further than it is right now. Just so you know, I'm going to be really pissed off if you think that I'm going to bow down before you and be your willing slave."

"I don't expect you to be my willing anything." He looked around again. "I'm still not sure this isn't a joke being played on us by my brothers. They've been teasing me a great deal about being the last one to get a mate."

"What are you anyway?" He told her that he was a light colored jaguar. "I don't know what that means either. Light colored?" He explained to her what he meant and how Rogen, his brother Weston's wife, was a dark jaguar. "I see, but that still doesn't mean that I want to be your slave. Or have anything to do with you at all."

"I don't blame you." He moved to get more of the furniture, and she let him. When he pulled off one of the last few pieces, she helped him load it on the trolley that they were using to get things up the front stairs. "I'm considered quite a catch by some of the women in town. Not that I have dated all that many of them. But that's what I heard."

"Like I care." Once he had it up the stairs, she went back to the truck to help with something else. He disappeared into the darkness of the house, and she tried her best to forget about him and being his mate. Like that was going to happen anytime soon.

When the truck was empty she closed the doors and waited for someone to sign off on the work order. She had to have someone sign it, or she didn't get paid. As he came out of the house, she noticed that he was better looking in the bright light of the moon. Not that she'd say that to him, but it was something that she could think about. Later, not tonight. She still had to go to the warehouse where she had to bring a load back from. And she was going to leave tonight if she had enough hours to go.

By the time he'd signed off on the paperwork, she was about as pissed off as she could be. Who the hell did he think he was telling her that she was his mate? She didn't need a man in her life, nor did she want one.

Getting in her truck to leave, she was stopped once again because she forgot to get the furniture blankets that had wrapped the things up that she'd brought. As she was pulling out of the driveway, she saw him staring at her through the side mirror. She wondered what he could be thinking and decided that she didn't care. As she'd told him, her life was fine just the way it was.

It took her less than an hour to get to the warehouse, where she was picking up a return load. Since they were closed up to loading, she decided to get into her bed and try to get a little rest. It wasn't as stressful as it used to be driving a big rig; she was getting used to it, but it did exhaust her when she had to help unload something like furniture.

She was just waking up when her cell phone rang. Groaning when she realized it was her father, she answered with her name and nothing more. He'd either be pissed off and hang up because she only said Rothchild, or he'd talk to her about whatever was going on in his life at the moment. She didn't want to talk to him today.

"I think I have the gout." She asked him what his symptoms were. "I don't have any that the internet says I should, but I know that I have it. It's in my feet. That's the most common one."

"What does it tell you to do to get rid of it? And so you know, I'm working right now and don't have time to go over all the symptoms that you might or might not have." He called her ungrateful. "Of course I am. Why do you even bother calling me when you have some kind of ailment?"

"I wish you were a son. He'd have more sympathy toward my illnesses." She said he had a son. "Well, he's busy working. What you do isn't work, Demi. It's a waste of time with your education that I paid for."

"You didn't pay anything for my education; I had scholarships. And I like this better than being a doctor in a place that doesn't appreciate me. Sort of like you don't." He sputtered around, calling her ungrateful again. "If I'm so ungrateful, why do you call me all the time? I'm sure you have better conversations with Liam and Dan."

"I do, but they don't have the wherewithal to help me when I have something wrong with me. You're just jealous because I love them more than I do you." He'd said that to her before. And while it still hurt deep in her heart, she didn't say anything to him about the pain he'd inflicted on her. "Did you hear me?"

"I heard you, and believe it or not, I don't care anymore. It's not like you're going to take out an ad in the newspaper about how much you dislike your daughter. And if you did, what good would that do you? None. If you have gout, which I don't believe that you do, then stop drinking, lower the acidic foods that you're eating, and see a real doctor, as this one is no longer going to be yours."

Hanging up on her father always felt good for about two seconds, then she felt terrible and wanted to call him back and tell him how sorry she was. She wouldn't. She'd done that once before, and all it had caused her was grief. Getting out of the truck to see when she was going to be loaded, she left her cell phone in the rig and walked the distance to the building to get her information.

By the time she was ready to leave with her load, she was pissed off again. They'd made her wait until noon even though she'd been at the door since eight in the morning. Getting her paperwork finished up, she was finally on her way at one in the afternoon and wondering how she was going to be able to make her truck payment without having to dip into her savings.

It couldn't be helped, she supposed. But then there was plenty of money in her account to pay off the truck; she just liked living on the edge. Laughing at herself, she was nearly to the next stop when her cell rang again. She didn't recognize the number, so she didn't answer. It would be just like her father to use someone else's phone just to trip her up.

Being off on the weekend made it so that she could go to her condo for a few days. She had plenty to do there, laundry and cleaning up her rig. She wasn't messy at all, but she did like to get her sheets washed when she could and clean the windows of the rig. They'd get really dirty when she was traveling. The windows, she told herself, not her sheets.

She'd nearly forgotten to check her messages when she got home. There were two from the estate that she'd picked up things from. They wanted her to take the next load to the client, and she was going to refuse. All she needed was to hang out with Jameson again so that he could begin his knocking her around as his slave. She had more important things to do, like going to the dentist rather than being around a jerky guy like him.

The next time her phone rang, she answered it

knowing that it was going to be either her father or her brothers. They would want something from her, and she'd turn them down, then they'd call her again. It was a never-ending thing with them, trying to get off the phone for one ailment or another that they claimed that they had. Answering the phone with a snarl of her name, she was surprised when the person at the other end laughed.

"It's Jameson Sheppard. You have wonderful phone manners." She asked him what he wanted. "They said that they're having trouble with the delivery of the rest of my stuff, and I was to call you and convince you to take the load. I have no idea why they thought that I could get you to do it, but I said that I'd try."

"It's my days off." He said that he was sorry and would get someone else to deliver it. "Never mind. I'm hiding from my family right now, so I'll go get it. I can have it for you, provided that it's loaded for you tomorrow morning. Will that suit you?"

"That's perfect. I'll have my brothers on standby to help again. They sort of owe me." She didn't want to ask, but found herself asking if it had been a joke, her being his mate. "No, that part is true. But we can talk about it when you get here."

"No, thanks. I told you that I don't want a mate at all, and that's the way it's going to be from now on." He didn't say anything, and she thought about the way she'd said it. No wonder she didn't have any friends, she thought that if that was the way she spoke to them all the time. "I'll be there tomorrow morning. We can talk if you want, but I'm not going to be your mate. As I said, I have better things to do with my life than to be a slave to some man who thinks I'm stupid."

"All right, we'll talk then. But I know you're not stupid, so I would never say that to you." When he hung up the phone, she felt angry. Then the guilt that she'd treated him like she had her father settled in. Christ, she thought, she was never going to be in a good mood for more than an hour at a time if she kept this up.

Before You Go...

HELP AN AUTHOR

write a review

THANK YOU!

Share your voice and help guide other readers to these wonderful books. Even if it's only a line or two, your reviews help readers discover the author's books so they can continue creating stories that you'll love. Log in to your favorite retailer and leave a review. Thank you.

AWARD WINNING, BESTSELLING AUTHOR

Kathi S. Barton is an award-winning and bestselling author known for her steamy paranormal romances and unforgettable characters. A recipient of the prestigious Pinnacle Book Achievement Award, her books have topped the charts on Amazon and All Romance eBooks, earning her a loyal global readership.

Kathi lives in Nashport, Ohio, with her husband, Paul. When she's not crafting passionate love stories set in magical worlds, she enjoys camping, exploring local auctions, and attending county fairs, where Paul showcases his artwork and pottery. Her creative spark—fueled by a muse she describes as a cross between Jimmy Stewart and Hugh Jackman—brings her stories to vivid, heartfelt life.

Paranormal romance with plenty of heat is her favorite genre, and she loves connecting with her readers. Feel free to reach out— Kathi would love to hear from you.

Email: aaronskiss@gmail.com
Blog: kathisbartonauthor.blogspot.com